Adolphus

Wolves of Rome Series Book 1

Scarlett J Rose

My eternal thanks to Susan Horsnell, my editor and all round kick-arse cheerleader, who pushed me to keep writing even when the times became so dark I wasn't sure I'd be able to pull myself out of the hole. There's always a light at the end of the tunnel, sometimes that tunnel is so long, the light is barely visible - but it is there.

Author's Note:

The world of the Roman Era was one which has been well documented, Scholars such as Julius Caesar himself documented their battles with the 'barbarian tribes' they encountered.

I have endeavoured to add to this world with Adolphus and Siglinds story.

Though the Suebi were a real tribe that were encountered by Caesar's Legions, I have used a little bit of creative licence when it came to the ceremonies and rituals, but always keeping in mind the documented rituals, and trying to stay as true as possible to recorded history.

This story, and those that follow it, follows the lives of four men, who were literally born into the Roman Legion. Their curse of Lycanthropy is a different take on the 'normal' types, (eg parents are werewolves, or they were bitten by one and thus become one) this is a curse of the Gods, but Rome, in all its wisdom interpreted it as a blessing for the military.

As much as I have tried to preserve the historical elements, this is a paranormal fiction, and as such I hope you enjoy it.

Chapter One:

Within the cold, dark room of a small *Lupinarium* in the slums of Rome, a whore panted as the pains of childbirth bit into her flesh. Her body shook with exhaustion from her hours-long labour. The midwife looked up at the stricken woman from between her parted knees.

"Push Clivia, you must push, now!" the old midwife urged.

Clivia's eyes darted to the Legate who stood silently watching her with the eyes of a predator as she lay in her most vulnerable position. He was the father of this child and his air of indifference for her condition brought fear into her heart.

She feared for her child and for herself, for what could a man with such an indifferent approach to the birth of his firstborn have planned for her and their child?

Clivia screamed and gripped the sweat-soaked linens in fisted hands as another contraction tore through her stomach. She pushed at the midwife's urging. She felt the baby shift its position as she forced the child out into the cold, cruel world. Her wailing scream and exhausted sobs were joined by the mewling and indignant cry of her child.

She sobbed with relief, it was over, done. Finished.

"A boy!" the midwife said with a smile as she held the squalling and bloody newborn aloft. Steam arose from his hot little body as the chill of the room met with his bloodied skin.

"Is he one of *them*?" The Legate asked from the shadows, his gravelly voice harsh and demanding.

The midwife cooed at the boy as she wiped him clean of his mother's fluids.

"Bring me the silver and we shall see."

The Legate approached, the white robes of his political office were clean against the drying blood that reached to the midwife's elbows. He handed the woman a trinket, a silver wolf's head. The midwife placed the silver against the meaty part of the baby's upper arm, just below his shoulder. The baby screamed in pain.

Clivia sat up, crying out her distress as her own body rebelled against the sudden movement so soon after childbirth.

"What are you doing? Don't hurt my son!" she cried out, struggling against the other women who had been nothing but shadows in her pain-filled world as she gave birth to her first child.

"Well?" the Legate prompted, ignoring the whore.

"The boy is one." The woman said, removing the offending silver from the boy's newly damaged skin.

The burns would scar, as the boy had yet to take on the blessing that Mars had bestowed on a select few boys born in this *Lupinarium* in Rome, on the very ground where Romulus had slain his brother, Remus, and spilled his blood, cursing the place where the *Lupinarium* stood.

This curse was considered a secret, a blessing for Rome and her soldiers. It offered them a chance to employ a specialised soldier when the sons of the *Lupinarium's* whores became young men.

Within each bastard son of a whore and a Roman soldier of repute or rank lay a sleeping wolf. On the first full moon after their thirteenth birthday, the dormant wolf rose to join the spirit and the flesh of the youth.

Their natural instinct and talent for hunting and scouting was employed by Rome's armies and the *Lupus Militum* were born. The Wolf Soldiers of Rome.

"He shall be called Adolphus," The Legate said as the midwife wrapped the boy in a clean cloth and handed him to the Legate's slave. He moved to the entryway of the whore's room, his slave bearing his bastard son behind him. "Deal with the whore," he ordered the two soldiers who stood guard outside.

The Legate did not stay to witness the final moments of Clivia's life. He had no regard for the woman whom he had lain with for months to ensure the boy's conception. He had done his duty to Rome and he knew his wife would understand, especially as she had been unable to provide him with a child. If she did not accept this bastard son of his, he would divorce her and find a young, fertile woman who would.

Clivia's panicked and desperate pleas for her son's return were cut off suddenly. The soldiers left soon after with a large bundle wrapped in blood soaked linens.

****

Twenty-two years later.

The stench of the campfires irritated his sensitive nose and stung his eyes as he ran the blade of his Gladius over the whetstone. The shine of his spit upon the rough stone glistened in the firelight as the conversation on the other side of the fire turned to him. He sat alone, apart from the other soldiers he would gladly call brother, if they were not such bastards.

"Hey, dog." Claudius called out loudly, gaining attention from others nearby as Claudius' friends around him snickered.

Adolphus didn't bother to respond.

"Dog, I'm talking to you." Claudius began whistling him as if he would demean himself before these fools and act like a common dog! He was a soldier of Rome and not a slave to use for their entertainment.

"Come on boy, there's a good boy!" Laelius patted his knees in a mockery of enticement.

"Hey, Dog, we were wondering - when you fuck a whore like your mother, do you do it as a wolf or a man?" Claudius sat chewing a piece of meat.

"Do you twist like a dog when you fuck a bitch? I bet that tickles your prick just right." Marius sniggered before he began to thrust his hips in a vulgar motion and whining and howling like a dog.

"I bet you fucked your own mother to get a curse like that." Claudius pushed.

Adolphus' wolf stirred, its fur bristling beneath his skin and the urge to shift and rip the fool's throat out, splattering his warm, tangy blood over his idiot friends was almost too good to pass up. Almost.

Adolphus knew they were goading him, he would not feel the lash ever again. He had promised himself after the last time they'd used the special, silver-tipped whip on him that he'd control the angry wolf which lay waiting for the chance to be free of the man's skin.

"No, actually, it was your mother whom I fucked, she was a real bitch too." he spoke casually while focused on sharpening his blade. He held the blade up to his face, checking the edge with his thumb and felt the sting as the sharp blade sliced through his skin before he licked the drops of blood from his flesh. The wound closed quickly and he looked at the trio. "Oh and your sisters, all of them, they lined up like bitches in heat for my cock, presenting their pretty pink cunts for me to defile. Even said I was much better than your tiny little prick, Claudius."

His own goading had the desired effect.

Claudius rose with a snarl, standing up to his full height. He was taller and broader than Adolphus, but Adolphus was quicker. Claudius had barely drawn his blade when Adolphus was there, his own blade pressed against the skin of his 'brother' soldier. A thin line of red appeared in the depression of skin where his blade met flesh, the iron biting deep enough to draw blood to the surface. Adolphus could smell the metallic scent of Claudius' blood.

"You would be wise to sit down, Claudius, and remember not to poke a wolf. We are wild creatures, wild and dangerous." He snarled before barking viciously into Claudius' face, his spittle flying through the air to land on Claudius's mouth and cheeks. The big man blanched and the stink of piss assailed his senses. Adolphus looked down to see Claudius' leather sandals had grown darker with the urine that trickled down his legs and puddled at his feet.

"If you piss yourself at my presence, I'd hate to see how you fare when facing the enemy." Adolphus grinned. "Perhaps you'll be known as Claudius the Piddler in the Legate's reports to Gaius Julius Caesar." He pulled the blade away, revealing the thin red line where the sharp blade had sliced lightly into Claudius' skin. "I'm sure General Caesar will reward you for your bravery, maybe you'll live forever in his next *Commentarii.*

He stepped around the fire and lowered himself back onto the log where he had been originally perched. He pulled out an oiled cloth and began to clean his Gladius.

The crunch of sandal on the dusty ground alerted him to the approach of their Legate. The man's unique scent was a dead giveaway.

Adolphus stood and turned. "Hail Legate Valerius." He fisted his right hand over his heart in a salute of respect to his General. The other soldiers behind him followed suit, standing to attention at the presence of their Legate. Valerius nodded to the other men before he focused on Adolphus.

"Hail Adolphus, I have orders for you."

"They must be important for you to deliver them to me yourself, Sir."

"Indeed. Come, let us adjourn to my pavillion, the orders are of a sensitive nature and I fear I do not trust my soldiers as I once did." He spoke in a low voice, his eyes darting over the soldiers by the fire.

Adolphus followed Legate Valerius through the bustling camp.

Valerius was a bulky man and often went without his armour while in camp. He'd had to have it resized many times due to his growing stomach. The man's insides seemed to be rotting as well and oftentimes Adolphus would catch the scent of Valerius' rotting teeth. Adolphus wondered as to the lavish lifestyle and foods he must have consumed to do such things to his body.

Soldiers worked to finish the repairs on their armour, or to work out the nicks in their Gladius'. The soft moans coming from other tents not too far away and the scent of females and sex indicated that other soldiers were working out their frustrations with the camp's followers.

Slaves scurried about, carrying out menial tasks with eyes downcast, their body language submissive,. One or two showed a slight defiance in their manner and Adolphus knew they would be punished severely by the lash for any transgressions.

This was life in the Roman Legions. Gaius Julius Caesar led their great campaigns and through his military genius, had raised the Roman flag on many new territories. His thirst for conquest rivalled that of Alexander the Great. Rome was fast becoming one of the greatest nations in the known world.

They arrived at the Legate's pavillion, two soldiers who stood guard at the entrance bowed their heads and saluted their general before one pulled aside the heavy flap of the tent's entrance and allowed the men to enter.

Adolphus' eyes took a moment to adjust to the dimness which suffused the interior of the pavillion. Candles flickered with their passing, the scent of tallow wax and the Legate's own scent permeated the atmosphere. Valerius moved further into the large pavillion, heading to a small section where a wooden desk sat upon a woven wool rug. He settled into a chair on the other side of the desk and pulled a scroll of parchment from a leather container. Valerius unrolled the scroll as Adolphus came to a stand before his Legate as he revealed the map that had been inked on the parchment. He placed small lead weights on each corner to hold the rolled map flat.

Before them, inked in intricate detail, was a map of the Germanic lands, those which they knew of.

"This is a scouting mission, you are not to engage with the native populace. Our Germanic allies, the Ubii, have given us reason to believe that members of this particular tribe of the Germanian Suebi are going to attack. Gaius Julius Caesar's own scouts have reported that there are approximately one hundred thousand Suebi scattered in encampments across the river, most of them are women and children. Apparently they've been promised new lands across the river by their king, Ariovistus. They are amassing an army within the forests here. Some have already crossed the river to join Ariovistus in a forward camp here." Valerius pointed to a large expanse of forest inked on the goatskin.

"There are several small villages nearby which will most likely be supplying the army with food. Your orders are to scout out each village and report back before the next full moon, sooner if you believe they are to march on our position. And of course, you are to use your 'special talents' to remain hidden." Valerius looked up as a slave girl brought over a jug of wine and a platter of fruit and cheese. The Legate grabbed the girl by the upper arm, startling her, before he pulled her down so her ear was by his mouth. He whispered for her to retire to the bedchamber and await him. The girl bowed her head and left the men.

Adolphus kept her in his field of vision, she moved past the partition into the Legate's bedchamber and began to disrobe. Naked she settled on the woven rug beside the Legate's cot to await him. The Legate caught Adolphus' glance and smirked, placing a hand on the younger man's shoulder.

"The privileges of rank, Adolphus. Work hard and rise up and you too will one day be in my position." Valerius poured them both a cup of wine, raising his in toast.

"*Ad victoriam*, Adolphus." he said before downing his drink.

"Ad victoriam, Legate Valerius." Adolphus replied, his eyes returned to the map, his mind on his mission.

Chapter Two.

Throughout the forest, Siglind's voice rang out in sweet song as she walked among the ancient trees. The great Birches standing like silent sentinels as she hunted for the fungi and herbs her Grandmother had requested. The song was old, sung to many a child by their mother, including Siggi and her older brother, Hallbjörn. Though their mother had passed into the afterlife many years ago, her spirit still visited Siggi as she dreamed.

Her grandmother had helped to raise her and her brother, their father was too busy for his children while attending to business with the Chieftain of their village. Siggi had become an apprentice to her Grandmother who was the village wisewoman and healer. If her mother had lived, it would have been her teaching Siggi the ways of the Gods' will and the powers they offered to their wisewomen.

Grandmother had started to succumb to the rigors of old age. On a good day, Edda was able to get out of bed and move about the small mud hut. Sometimes, to even venture outside without the aid of her granddaughter. But today was not a good day. The old woman's body was tired and her limbs refused to move with the strictures of age. Edda knew what fate awaited her, and that her time would be soon, but she was determined to finish Siggi's training before the Gods called to her to join them.

Siggi plucked a few more fungi from the ground and placed them in the woven reed basket she carried, adding to the small pile of fungi and mugwort she'd collected. The lonesome sound of a wolf's mournful howl echoed through the forest. Her long, braided hair shifted along her back as she turned to look around. A few errant stands tickled her cheeks and fell over her breasts, catching the dappled sunlight and shining golden as she glanced around. The wolf's call was distant, but she knew a wolf could run quite fast, much faster than she could. Normally, fear would be coursing through her body on hearing a wolf's call. But there was something in this creature's mournful lament that brought her comfort, not fear.

Their legends spoke of Wolves devouring the sun and moon, heralding the end times and the destruction which would be wrought by the great wolf Fenrir, but Wotan himself had wolves as pets. Edda had told her never to fear the wolf, they were omens that could be both good or bad, but only the Gods could know their meaning.

Siggi moved quickly through the forest, heading back towards the village. The smoke from the cook fires as she neared her home gave the forest a hazy ambiance and the familiar sights and smells of the village grew stronger as she approached. She felt safer, although she heard the call of the wolf once more before she broke through the treeline and walked across the small field where the village's goats grazed.

"Siggi!" Ingulf called out to her from his perch on an old tree stump. "What have you got? Did you find any blackberries?" The young boy leapt from his seat and raced over to her, his blue eyes shining with hope.

"No Ing, I'm sorry, but I only have the fungi that Edda asked me to get, besides it is far too early in the season for berries, even you know that."

"When it is time will you let me come with you to collect them?" Ingulf asked.

"Of course." Siggi smiled, tousling the boy's hair. "Now you best tend to those goats, and don't let them stray too far. I heard wolfsong in the forest, so there may be a hunting pack nearby."

Ingulf's eyes widened and the boy clutched his dagger by the hilt. "I'll keep the wolves away, don't you worry Siggi. I want to be a great warrior someday.

"I know you will, Ing."
Ingulf scuffed his bare feet in the dirt, looking down before he shyly looked up at her.

"Siggi, when will you see my future?"

"When Edda thinks I'm ready. I've not finished my training yet, but you'll be one of the first, I promise." She reached up and ruffled his hair. "You must have patience, you cannot rush the Gods any more than you can rush a mountain." She smiled before she turned and continued through to the village.

Hallbjörn was waiting for her by the first of the village's huts, leaning against the mud and thatch wall as he chewed on a piece of dried meat. Her brother's ready smile and good looks often had the young women of the village after him for marriage, or even a simple roll in the furs. Halli, as he was known to their family and friends, was more interested in securing his place in Valhalla than securing a wife who would only grieve him when his time came to enter the realms of the Gods.

"That boy dotes on you, you know. His little heart will break when Kurst comes courting you."

"I have no interest in Kurst." Siggi spoke as she continued to walk past her brother. "He is a fool if he thinks he can court me. He is an oaf and a braggart who thinks his feats in battle will bring any woman to his bed." She spun to face her brother. "I am not any woman."

"I know, sweet sister." Her older brother smiled as he fell into step with her. "You are Siglind, and you will be a great wisewoman." He put an arm around her shoulders and pulled her against his side.

"I only hope that the Gods will give me guidance to help our tribe." She admitted as they walked towards Edda's hut on the far side of the village.

"I'm sure they will. We will need that guidance in the coming weeks if we are to be victorious against the Ubii and their Roman allies."

"These Romans, I have heard tales they are a very powerful people. Do you think we can stand against them again, Halli?"

Hallbjörn was quiet for a moment as they walked. His brow furrowed as he thought over the question. "With the Gods on our side, I don't think we can lose."

"If you spoke with more confidence, I might believe you, brother." Siggi said as they passed the village's longhouse, where their father sat in counsel with their Elder. "Do you speak your heart or that of our father?"

"Do you doubt the Gods, my sister?"

"No, I do not doubt the Gods. They guide us in everything." Siggi sighed and looked down at the basket in her hands, needing to move on from the discomforting accusation.

"Then what is on your mind, sister?"

"Edda has been having dreams, disquieting ones." She looked to the end of the path where the water of their small river glittered in the late afternoon sun. A short distance beyond the last homes lay Edda's hut.

"And these dreams give you cause to doubt our victory?"

"She hasn't spoken of them, but I hear her talk in her sleep. She speaks of wolves and a plague that will sweep across our lands like blood. I heard a wolf in the forest this day and perhaps I make more of it than there truly is, but wolves are the harbingers of the end times and I fear it may be upon us soon."

"We can only hope the chieftain will heed the words of the Gods, whatever they say." Her brother placed a hand on her shoulder.

Siggi nodded.

"The Chieftain will listen to the King and it is he who should heed the words and signs of the Gods." She sighed, looking down at the basket in her hands "I best be going, it does not bode well to dwell on dark times and Edda will be waiting for me. I think I will ask her to consult the Oracle and ask for guidance."

"Be careful, sister, and may Wotan guide you."

"And you, brother."
The siblings parted ways.

****

Siggi ambled through their village to Edda's mud hut, passing clucking chickens and pigs which wandered through their home.

Come winter, most people would huddle in the longhouse for warmth along with their animals, abandoning their simple homes during the cold winter nights to enjoy the warmth of the Chieftain's hearthfire.

She pushed open the door to Edda's hut, a gust of chilled wind followed her.

"Gods, close the door girl, before the wicked spirits come to drag me to the underworld!" Her grandmother's voice crackled hoarsely from within the gloom.

"They would never take you, Edda, you are far too strong and stubborn." Siggi smiled at the older woman as she pushed the door shut, banishing the cold from the old Seeress' home.

"Bah! Not as strong as you, my girl." The old woman settled into furs by the hearth, poking at the flames with a stick. "Did you bring me the mushrooms?" She turned in her nest to look over at her granddaughter.

"Yes, Edda." Siggi smiled as she unpacked the mugwort "And I found some Mugwort." She lifted the fronds for her grandmother to see in the warm glow of the tallow candles in the hut.

"Excellent, brew the leaves into a tea for me and bring me a few of those mushrooms. The Oracle calls me to seek her wisdom."

"The Oracle or the chieftain?" Siggi handed Edda a few of the thin, white mushrooms.

"Bah, the Chieftain is a fool. He won't listen to the ghosts of the past." Edda popped a few mushrooms into her mouth and chewed.

"Halli spoke to me about having the Gods on our side against the Romans. I told him I'd ask you to seek the Oracle's guidance in this." Siggi wrapped the skirt of her dress around her hand and used it to grab the iron kettle from over the fire. She added more water from a bucket and took out a bronze knife to prepare the leaves.

"I will ask the Oracle, but you know as well as I do, girl - the Oracle will only reveal what it wants us to know."

"Yes, Edda."
The old woman watched while Siglind busied herself with brewing her tea. Edda was quiet for a while, as the mushrooms brought on the vision.

Chapter Three.

Adolphus had made a small camp in a cave by a waterfall which fed a small tributary river that ran to the Rhine, where the rest of his brother soldiers camped, preparing for the coming battle. He had crossed the Rhine on a crude raft which had been cobbled together with timber considered unsuitable for the walls of the fortified Roman camp. Much of his spare clothing had become damp with the craft's poor construction, allowing water to seep through the timber boles at his feet as he poled his way across. The craft had survived the crossing, though the Gods only knew how.

He had trekked through the forest until the banks of the river and the Roman camp were far from sight before he unshouldered his pack and took a good, long look around the area. He then removed his clothing and stood as naked as the day the Gods had brought him into this world. The wolf scar on his arm itched and he absently scratched at it as he secured his armour and undergarments into his pack. His Gladius within easy reach, should he require it.

Adolphus stood away from his pack and gave his body over to his wolf. The beast within whined with anticipation as it was released from the cage of man-flesh that bound him, becoming one with the spirit of the man, his senses blending with that of his human form to become keener. Bones broke and were remoulded from human to lupine form. His nose elongated to a fine snout, his ears shifted to the top of his skull as it too elongated to accommodate its new form. Sharp canines were reformed from his existing teeth and his tongue lolled out between his grinning jaws. Fingers shortened into thick pads as fur, grey as a stormy sky, erupted from his pale skin to cover what was once the body of a man. Now, upon all fours, stood a proud wolf.

He nosed the pack into a position where he could easily slide it onto his back. With the pack secured, he'd bolted into the dense forest, his nose following the scent of a week-old trail, revealing the Romans had already been spied on by their enemy.

Adolphus felt the soft forest floor underneath the pads of his four paws. The chill wind of the north shifted the long, thick fur on his shoulder. The scents of a settlement filled his nostrils and the wolf lowered his head to the ground to track the Suebi woman whom he had seen briefly through the thick trees of the forest which surrounded the Suebi village.

He'd run for hours before he'd heard her singing. A clear, beautiful voice that carried through the trees. The birds singing, hidden within their green branches, accompanied her, though they fell silent when he approached. He couldn't help but join her in wolfsong. Something in his wild heart called to her. He could scent her fear in the wind. He called to her again, his long soulful cry caused the man within him to want to break free of the wolf and find this woman. To hold her, and mount her as a man as he could not do as a wolf. He scented her again, her fear rising, the stink of it corrupting the sweetness of her.

He paced quickly through the forest, tracking her movements. He caught a glimpse of hair shining like gold in the scattered light of the sun. She carried a basket woven of water reeds, the scent of strange fungi and freshly picked mugwort carried to his nose. The wolf watched as she broke through the forest into a clearing and spoke with a boy who tended a small herd of goats on the outskirts of the village.

He followed her movements as another male joined her, speaking to her and placing an arm around her shoulders. The wolf growled with jealousy. Within his soul, his wild heart, he knew the woman was his. His mate. It was as if Mars himself had given him the precious gift of his own Venus, a Goddess trapped in a mortal body - a woman of beauty and love. He watched as she left the other man and headed to a hut where the scent of an older woman drifted on the winds. When his woman opened the door, the scents of drying herbs and medicines drifted on the air to him. He considered who she was. A woman of healing, a wise woman, perhaps? Though she was very young to be considered a wise woman, perhaps she was in training?

He sniffed the ground a moment longer, desperate to catch another glimpse of her, before he turned and retreated back into the forest. He knew he had other villages to scout, but this one, he would be returning to and quite eagerly.

****

Edda lay upon the straw and fur covered bedding. Her breathing heavy and her lips dry as she spoke to the Oracle of the Gods in near nonsensical words. Siglind waited patiently, several sacred willow rods in hand ready to read and confirm the will of the Gods once Edda returned from her vision.

The old grandmother's eyes slowly became clear as she returned from the otherworld.

"Edda." Siggi leaned forward and offered her the bowl of tea. "Here, drink."

Edda's hands trembled as she took a steadying sip of the mugwort tea. She smacked her lips together after she swallowed the bitter brew.

'A pity we cannot add honey to it," she muttered before nodding to the willow rods in Siggi's hand. "Help me up, girl. The Gods are not within my simple home, nor should they be, though they are always welcome at my hearth."

Siggi helped Edda to her feet, covering her shoulders with a fur cape and grabbing the gnarled, but smooth birchwood staff Edda used to get around when her bones weren't chilled to uselessness. She opened the door for her grandmother and helped her to the stool her brother had made. She prepared the earth at her grandmother's feet, placing branches of sage in a circle around Edda, so no ill spirits would disturb the casting of the willow rods.

Edda held the willow rods in her gnarled hands.

"Oh Wotan, give us guidance, let us know your will. May the Gods and Goddesses of our people grant us the power to do as you will." Her voice cracked slightly on the last words as she held her hand out and dropped the willow rods.

The thin, dried twigs of willow wood dropped to the ground below. Cast by the old hand of the seeress and influenced by the Norns, the willow rods scattered within the circle of sage branches.

Edda's rheumy eyes read the signs.

"Wotan has given our request over to his son, Thor, who demands a sacrifice of flesh and blood at the dark of the moon. If it is pleasing to him, we shall be victorious, but if a bad spirit enters our homes or our sacred places, all will fail and a great darkness will sweep our lands."

Siglind shivered with Edda's declaration. She had seen the demand for blood and the warning of darkness in the way the rods had fallen. Edda pushed hard on the walking stick and rose on unsteady feet. "It is best we begin to prepare for the sacrifice." She hobbled towards her hut. "Go to your father and inform him of the God's will."

"Yes, Edda." Siggi, quickly gathered the sage and tossed it into the small brazier which sat smouldering with coals before Edda's doorway. She hoped the sacred herb would ward off any ill spirits that might be lurking.

Her mind drifted to the wolf and its mournful call as she had returned to the village. She wondered if it was a herald of a bad spirit, or if it had come to warn her of the darkness.

She moved quickly through the village and entered the longhouse, where within, the Chieftain and her father sat in consul with the other elder warriors.

The men sat around the hearth, drinking and telling stories of battles past. Of women they'd wooed and great victories in hunts against fearsome beasts. She approached slowly, the firelight casting shadows into the darker reaches of the longhouse.

Her father sat beside the Chieftain. Halli sat beside their father and on the other side sat the Chieftain's son, Kurst - A man she despised.

Kurst's eyes roamed her body, his slimy tongue slid out between his fleshy lips and ran over them. His look was hungry, predatory and turned her stomach. She ignored him, moving to focus her attention on the Chieftain.

"Forgive me, Chieftain." She bowed her head in respect for their leader. "But I bring news from Edda and the Oracle.

"What is it, Siglind?" the Chieftain asked, his tone showing his irritation with the interruption.

"The Gods, Wotan and Thor, demand a sacrifice." She spoke solemnly. The men were quiet after she made the proclamation of the God's will. "On the dark of the moon, we shall all gather at the sacred grove and a sacrificial meal of two goats will be consumed by the people. There, our warriors will be blessed for the coming conflict with our enemies."

"Is that all?" the Chieftain asked.

"Yes, Lord." Siggi bowed her head again.

"Then you may go. We will make preparations and let everyone know." He dismissed her with a wave of his hand. She turned and walked out of the longhouse, relieved to be away from Kurst's covetous stare.

Chapter Four

Adolphus sat in the chill of the night and watched from his hiding place, naked in his human form, as the procession of Suebi villagers moved through the forest and towards the marshy bog. Soft wisps of smoke drifted over the group of warriors who wore animal fur, with the heads still attached, as cloaks and villagers who carried baskets of millet, root vegetables and dried grains. The beautiful young Suebi maiden he had seen and whom his wolf had claimed, walked beside a small and simply made litter, borne by four strong Suebi warriors, upon which an old woman rested. Flickering torchlight held in the hands of the leading warriors guided the way. Others held torches entwined with burning dried sage leaves aloft to chase away the darkness and evil spirits that might lurk within the gloom.

Two bleating goats were led by warriors dressed for war, their weapons glinting against the flickering torchlight. The scent of burning sage, juniper and lavender drifted on the wind. Soft chanting reached his ears and the sweet alto of her voice was clear amongst the baritone of the men. From what he understood of the Germanic tongue being spoken here, they were imploring their Gods for guidance.

Adolphus had travelled through the forest, finding several small camps and villages that were growing with the influx of Suebi warriors and villagers from other parts of the Suebi's lands. The threat to their Roman camps and settlements along the Rhine was growing, the Suebi were fearless and relentless in battle. Adolphus knew in his bones there was going to be a great battle between the Suebi and his people. He prayed to Mars that he could help turn the tide in their favour

Each eve he returned to his cave and proceeded to write down his reports. In a few days, he would return to an old tree on the banks of the river Rhine and place the sealed leather container with the parchment paper reports within the knotted hole in the tree's gnarled old trunk for one of the Legion's other scouts to retrieve and take to Valerius.

But for now, he watched and followed the chanting procession on silent paws after shifting back to his wolf, lest he be seen in his human form.

They reached a small clearing in the forest, not far from the bog. Here the warriors unbound their hair and washed their hands and faces in a bowl of water provided by the golden-haired beauty he was so drawn to. He wanted to know everything about her; the softness of her hair on his bare chest, the scent of her sweat after lovemaking, the soft sounds she would make as he took her, the swell of her belly as she bore his children. His human body stirred under the wolf's fur. He instinctively knew the Fates had given him this beautiful creature as his mate, the other half of his soul which had been taken by the Gods when he was born and cast to the world to seek another body until they could be bound back together.

The group of warriors finished cleansing their hands and faces and sat in a line, waiting. The old woman was settled down before them and held aloft a smouldering bundle of herbs. She chanted to her Gods, imploring them to care for their warriors in the coming battle and if they fell, she asked that they find their place in the afterlife. She handed the smouldering bundle to his girl and he watched as she passed the smouldering stick over the men's heads. She was followed by two women, each one began to comb the warrior's hair over to the side of his head and worked the long tresses into a Suebi Knot, an intricate styling that was distinctive to the Suebi tribes.

He noticed one male in particular watched his little mate with covetous eyes and a lustful stare. He growled low and deep, showing displeasure at another male desiring what the gods had given him.

Once the last knot was tied, the warriors rose and followed his mate out of the clearing and into the bog. Adolphus followed, his paws squelching softly in the soft and muddy earth. They came to a place which was filled with animal skulls stuck atop long sticks. Two large wooden totems made from the upside-down trunks of oak trees dominated the clearing. In the wood were carved faces and runic symbols stood at the head of the circle of skull totems. She waved the stick over the two large totems before laying it between the 'feet' of the Gods' idols where the wisps of smoke rose towards the night sky.

The goats were brought forward and held by a warrior while his female chanted and praised her Gods before she lifted a bronze knife and slit the animal's throats, spilling their blood before the feet of the totems. She quickly caught the blood from the gaping throats of the animals in clay bowls, waiting until the last drops had fallen from the sacrificial beasts and their bodies had been guided to the ground by the hands of two young men. Behind her, villagers had gathered dried peat and wood and were starting a fire on a small and rare section of dry land.

He watched as his mate dipped her fingers into the blood and began to paint symbols on the smooth wood of the oak boles.

She turned with the bowl in hand and waited for the warriors to kneel in a semi-circle around her. Two villagers began to skin and butcher the animals. His mate dipped her fingers in the blood again and flicked it over the faces of the warriors, painting them with splatters of crimson. Another villager brought forth a clay jug, the creamy scent of cows' milk drifted over the tang of fresh blood and smoke from the fire and smouldering herbs. She mixed the milk in with what remained of the blood, the liquid turning pink as the creamy milk mixed with the crimson blood. She held the bowl aloft and spoke, beseeching a blessing from the Gods before she turned and offered the bloody milk to the first warrior. He placed his scarred hands over hers and drank from the bowl before she offered it to the next warrior in line, repeating the process with each kneeling warrior.

Behind them, the villagers were cooking the meat. The scent of roasting goat made Adolphus hungry and he knew he had to hunt, but he was far too entranced with the beautiful woman who looked even more glorious in the rising firelight. She looked up, her eyes seeming to connect with him in the darkness. She stared at him for a moment, before seemingly gathering herself and returning her attention to the ceremony.

Within that moment, he felt the connection strengthen. He knew he had to have her, but by Mars, how was it to be?

Chapter Five

Siglind felt the eyes of a wolf upon her as she placed the offering of millet and dried fruits into the mud of the bog. She wondered if the creature was a Familiar of Wotan and if so, she hoped their sacrifices on this night pleased him. She knew elsewhere within the depths, other, more human sacrifices lay at rest within the muddy depths. Behind her, the men and women of her village ate the cooked meat, along with bread and vegetables, in a sacrificial meal dedicated to the Gods. They hoped they may gain strength for this coming battle.

She knew soon her people would join King Ariovist across the river. The Romans posed a threat to their battle against their enemies, the Ubii, who had allied themselves with the feared Romans.

The Suebi were a warlike race. They often waged war with their neighbours over hunting territories, or incursions into their own lands, believing they were the greater, more powerful tribe in the area. For that arrogance, perhaps the Gods might turn their eyes from the Suebi. It was one of her greater fears, and tonight Siggi prayed and sacrificed against that possibility.

As the tribe ate, Edda called Siglind to her side. The old grandmother sat upon a fur-lined litter which four of their brave warriors had carried. Her father had led the way beside their Chieftain, bright flickering torches held aloft. Siggi had kept a smouldering smudge stick of sweet lavender, cleansing sage, mugwort and sweetgrass, weaving the smoke through the air to ward off any bad spirits. The men would dream of their battles tonight as they ate the sacrificial meal. Already she could see the cleansing smoke having an effect.

She felt her own eyes drifting closed as she too gave into the will of the Gods.

The lonesome howl of a wolf called to her within the haze of her smoke-induced dreams. She wandered through the woods until she came across the waterfall they called Freyja's Tears. It was one of their sacred places. At the base was a pool and along the cliffs, just before the pool, was a cave. Her bare feet carried her towards the clear pool where the water fell, misting before it joined the rippling pool.

At the cave's entrance sat a grey wolf, his eyes bright and as blue as the clear winter sky. He howled again, his song calling her, urging her to come to him. As she watched, he shimmered and changed, forming a naked man, the most handsome she had ever seen. His hair was dark, his eyes the same clear blue as the wolf's. He held a hand out to her, beckoning her to join him with a playful smile. She smiled back at him, suddenly shy, but intrigued.

"Come, join me, it is meant to be. You are mine, as I am yours." His voice carried a strange accent. She reached out to him and took his hand. He led her into the cave where he had obviously been camping. Two rabbits hung from the roof and a small bag of grain lay beside his metal cooking pot. He brought her to his sleeping mat and carefully undressed her until she stood naked as he. Her body warmed at the simple but sweet caresses that he reverently gifted her with.

He leaned forward and pressed his lips against her bare shoulder, brushing aside the golden braids of her hair to find her skin. His hands, rough from years of wielding a weapon, grazed against her body as he moved behind her. His fingers, calloused and careworn brushed roughly against her breasts, causing her body to tingle with anticipation of where he might just place his hands next. Her soft sighs of pleasure grew as his hands explored her body - from neck, to breast, down her stomach and finally to the curls of hair between her thighs.

Her wolf-man slid his fingers leisurely through her curls before sliding them slowly into the slickness he had aroused at her sex. His warm breath was soft, puffing against her shoulder as he pressed himself against her back. The thickness of his manhood pushed against the seam of her buttocks and with a firm hand on her shoulder, he brought her to her hands and knees. The heat of his body flush against her back as he reached between them and positioned his cock between her thighs, the head pressing urgently against her opening.

Normally, she would have been reluctant to give herself to some stranger, but caught within the dream-smoke, she felt inexplicably drawn to this man as if it were truly demanded by the Gods that she let him mount her. She moaned softly as he took her, his thick cock pushing inside and resting there a moment before he began to thrust. Leaning back, his hands gripped her hips and he began to thrust with animalistic grunts that she found more stimulating than she could ever have imagined. Her own body responded to the gentle caresses he made to her hips and buttocks.

Her body tightened as the pleasure of the intimate act rushed through her body. His grunts and growls echoed through the small cave, her fingers curled into the elk fur beneath her. She began to pant and moan with each stroke of his manhood, the heat of his body at her backside grew and she could feel him swelling inside her as he raced towards the glorious ending of their rutting. His fingers slid over her hip and around to the apex of her thighs, he ran a thick finger through her curls and found a spot that made her toes curl and her voice cry out in delight as she fell through Midgard and found the realms of pleasure.

Siglind awoke, groggy and with memories of her coupling with the wolf-man still clear in her mind. She found herself slick between her legs and looked around at the slumbering warriors. Edda sat with wizened eyes watching her granddaughter.

"Siglind." she said, reaching over and caressing her granddaughter's cheek. "Do not fear the grey wolf. He will lead you to safety from the darkness. There will be a great and terrible price, but he will be there for you in the end, always remember this."

"Yes, Edda." She replied, shaken by the power of such a sexual dream.

Chapter Six

Siglind watched as her brother and the warriors of their clan left for the crossing camp. More of their tribe would join the camp and cross to join King Ariovist on the other side of the river. Many wives and children escorted them to the war camp. Only the very old and very young were left behind for now, with five warriors to protect them. As soon as these warriors were needed, word would be sent for those who remained behind to join them.

The warriors stood with packs slung over their backs, shields attached. Their weapons had been sharpened, farewells and wishes for good fortune in battle had been spoken to wives and family. King Ariovist was preparing to attack the Romans on the other side of the river and push them from the lands he had claimed for his people. There were many members of the Suebi waiting for their new lands as Ariovist had promised and now, Ariovist had called for more men to join the war camp and their clan had answered.

Edda watched from her stoop as Siglind bid her father and brother goodbye. When her granddaughter returned to her side, the old woman handed her a pack. Siggi knew she would have to leave and join the war host. As a wise woman in training, there were other wise women in the camp whom she could learn from. Although Edda was highly respected amongst their tribes as a great and powerful seeress, there were always many aspects of their craft to learn.

"Soon it will be time for you to take my place, Siggi," the old woman said.

"Edda, you still have years left." Siggi settled down beside her grandmother.

"Bah, flatterer." Edda emitted a derisive snort. "No, I feel the call of the Gods, little one. I'll be with your mother and her father soon." She stared down at the willow rods that were settled at her feet. She'd done a casting while the warriors were leaving.

"Edda... do you see darkness in the casting? Did you not use the sage leaves?" Siglind studied the omen in the rods.

"Aye, I do and I did indeed use the sage leaves. You need to prepare, for you will take my place sooner than we think, if the prophecy the rods have shown are correct." She leaned back, hands clasping the gnarled walking stick. "Time is running out, for all of us. A foul spirit will descend upon us, it will bring death. You should go to Freyja's tears for the Goddess will guide you." She pushed the pack closer.

"But who will care for you?"

"I am a grown woman, I can still do what I need to. Besides, young Ingulf offered to do the heavy lifting and bring wood and peat into my hearth."

Siglind sighed as her grandmother stood shakily.

"I'll send word to Wendelgard to seek you out at Freyja's Tears in a few days time. Now, go and may the Gods guide you."

Siggi shouldered her pack and headed to the river, the soft leather of her boots sank slightly into the soft earth beneath her feet. The trickle of the water was soothing and musical beside her as the shallow waterway trickled over the smooth rocks.

She walked for hours, the shadows lengthening as the warm spring sunshine drew the darkness from the trees. She drew her bow when she spotted a rabbit nibbling at some sweetgrass, saying a prayer to the Gods of the hunt before she loosed the quiver. The animal squeaked as the arrow struck it down. The rabbit still twitched as she approached.. Siggi thanked the creature for its gift of meat and fur before she cleanly snapped its neck and tied its hind feet to the leather belt at her hips.

The day was nearing its end when she arrived at the waterfall. Siglind dropped her pack and knelt at the pool, cupping her hands to drink the cool, clear water.

She set to skinning the rabbit and prepared a small fire to cook it over before setting up the small hide shelter Edda had packed for her. It was a simple piece comprising two deer-hides stitched together with animal gut. She gathered three good, solid branches to prop the leather over, using bone pins to secure the leather to the top branch in a loop and stones from the river at the end of the pool to weigh down the ends of the shelter so the wind would not blow it away. The rabbit was beheaded and set over the fire to cook, she kept the innards aside in a small wooden bowl. She'd done a short divination with them before and was pleased with the answer. She would be safe here.

The darkness was almost complete, the moon was at its half-crest and the stars blazed across the sky. Her ancestors were surely watching over her from their heavens.

Siggi saw a movement to the edge of her small camp. A flash of grey fur and a flicker of eyes reflecting in the light of the fire.

A wolf.

A grey wolf had come to visit. Siggi stayed still as the wolf watched from just beyond the fire's light. Remembering Edda's words, she moved slowly and respectfully, letting the Wolf come to her camp. His head was lowered and his tail still. Siggi very slowly leaned over and picked up the rabbit's guts. She pulled the little heart from the bloody mess and gently tossed it towards the wolf. It landed between his great paws.

The wolf looked at the bloody bit of flesh and sniffed it, before devouring the tiny heart and waiting, his tongue slipping out between his jaws and licking his lips as he eyed the bowl of innards.

"You wish for more, wolf?" Siggi smiled. "Where is the rest of your pack? I don't have enough for all of them."

The wolf seemed to listen to her and howled mournfully, his head tipped back, sending his song to the Gods. There were no others who returned his call. It echoed through the forest behind him and rebounded off the cliff walls behind her own camp. Siggi picked up the bowl and got to her feet slowly, taking the offering towards the wolf.

He looked at her warily. She placed the bowl halfway between her fire and where the wolf sat with his ice-blue eyes on her. He was seemingly wary of the woman, but something else shone behind them - a high intelligence, a strange desire that she couldn't name. She left the bowl and returned to her place by the fire, watching the wolf as he inched closer to the offering, , one hesitant step at a time, his eyes always on her.

Siggi watched as he moved the last few steps and lowered his nose to the bowl, sniffing it. "Go on, wise one," she urged him. "It's just rabbit." She smiled as the beast opened his jaw and devoured the rabbit's innards in a few hearty bites. The wolf licked the bowl clean and then his lips, which had a small smear of blood on them from the humble meal she had offered him. He lowered his head and padded towards the cliffs that rose from the lush ground to host the waterfall of Freyja's tears. Siggi wondered if he was the same wolf who had called to her in the forest not so long ago… perhaps he was the wolf from her dreams.

Chapter Seven.

Adolphus watched her from the dark of the cave as she set the head of the rabbit on a stick by the shore of the pool. In the dim light of the half-moon, she was ethereal, goddess-like in her movements. He had shifted back to his human form and was now sporting a painful erection. His ice blue eyes watched as she stripped and bathed in the cold waters of the pool and then returned, naked, to the fire to dry off before she dressed in her Suebi gown. She burned more herbs in a smudge stick, waving the smouldering bundle in an intricate pattern, perhaps to ward off evil spirits or animals from her camp, before she lay down in her furs and drifted off to sleep.

Adolphus shifted back to wolf form, part of him wasn't sure about approaching her in his human form just yet, but he yearned for the moment his hands could caress her skin. To feel her body beneath his, as he knew it should be, as the Fates placed their paths together and the Gods demanded. He felt an overwhelming need to protect her, to keep her from harm.

He slowly stalkled out of the cave and into the open. The light moonlight lending his grey fur a silver shade. He lowered his head to the ground, sniffing for any strange scents. All he could sense was his own musk.

Adolphus padded around her camp, sniffing, scenting and marking places to add to her own wards. His leg lifted against many trees and rocks, pissing to mark his space, lest any other predators come to attack his woman as she slept. Satisfied she would be safe this night, Adolphus turned and ran into the forest, he needed to hunt. A few measly rabbit's innards were not enough to satisfy the hunger of both man and wolf, he needed something more substantial.

He hunted throughout the night, bringing his fresh kills of a goose and a rabbit to her camp just as the dawn was causing the eastern sky to blush crimson.

He settled down on his belly and placed his head on his paws, dozing by the remnants of her fire while she slept in her shelter not too far from him.

****

Siglind slowly came awake to birdsong and the soothing sound of the waterfall. She opened her eyes to see the wolf had slept by her fire and he'd also brought her breakfast. She picked up the dead goose by the long, elegant and bloody neck and eyed the sleeping wolf. Siggi smiled at the beautiful gift. She set about plucking the bird, setting aside the stiff flight feathers for the fletchers in the camp, the down she placed in a small leather bag. The bird's head joined the rabbit's from the previous night, set on a stick as a spiritual totem for the Gods, so they might grant her wisdom in her journey and protection from harm. They were small sacrifices, but she was only one woman. One woman and a lone wolf.

Beside her, the wolf snuffled and sneezed, his fangs stark white against the pink of his gums. She smiled at the scrunched up grimace on his face.

"Good morning to you too," she said as she gutted the bird and placed the gizzards into the wooden bowl he'd eaten from the night before. Siggi spitted the bird and stoked up the fire, letting it cook slowly while she renewed the protection wards with the remains of her smudge stick. She felt the wolf's eyes on her, watching as she asked for the blessings of protection and guidance from the Gods. She returned to the fire, turning the bird so it would cook evenly.

The scent of the cooking goose was thick as its natural fats melted and dripped into the fire. She unwrapped a cloth which held her travel rations of bread and goats cheese and tore a chunk from the small loaf, before she took out her small bronze dagger and cut a piece off the cheese. She cut another piece and offered it to the wolf. He eyed her warily.

"It's all right, I won't hurt you. Besides, you're going to have to help me eat this goose." She smiled, shifting forward to offer the cheese. The wolf watched her with eyes that seemed so familiar, so *human*, if that were even possible. His snout moved closer to the offering, nose sniffing. She could feel the short puffs of breath on her fingertips before his warm, wet tongue slid over them. With utmost care and gentleness, he took the cheese from her fingers, not snatching it like she'd expect a wolf would do. She barely felt the brush of his teeth against her fingers as he accepted the offering. She watched with satisfaction as the wolf ate the cheese from her hand.

"There now, that wasn't so difficult, was it?" Siggi kept her hand out, fingers uncurled. The wolf eyed her outstretched hand, and then turned its gaze to her eyes, a look of trust seemed to grow within their icy depths. He inched forward on his paws, his large body brushing against the dirt, sticks and leaves carpeting the ground of the camp. He slowly, almost cautiously, pressed his nose against her hand, before he shuffled closer and the soft fur of his head rubbed against her hand.

Siggi slowly turned her hand so she could properly caress the strong head of the wolf. She ran her fingers up over his ears and down the back of his neck. The wolf shuffled forward a little more, until his head was in her lap.

It felt so natural to her, to have him snuggled up against her. His contented sighs and the soft wagging of his tail were comforting. In all her life, Siggi had never expected a wild wolf to behave in such a way. She looked up at the waterfall -Freyja's Tears. The soft rainbow colours which appeared in the mists seemed to be more than magical to her. The natural sounds of the forest surrounded them and it seemed like the Goddess herself was here. The wolf snuggled against her, in what she felt was an affectionate way. Siggi found her hands resting on his back, caressing and patting the wolf's soft coat.

"I wonder, if you are the one who came to me in my dreams?" She sighed. "But, that would be impossible, you'd have to turn into an attractive man for *that* dream to come true." She sighed again.

The wolf's tail wagged and he chuffed, as if laughing.
They sat there together for most of the morning, while the goose slowly cooked.

Chapter Eight.

Adolphus had enjoyed Siggi's comforting touch far too much and now he knew he had to leave her as his duty to Rome called. With an indignant huff he pushed himself to all fours and trotted out of the camp. Siggi called him, but he knew he could not go back to her, not just yet. He padded through the forest, his four paws crushing the leaf matter underfoot. He'd travelled for miles but the scents of the distant crossing camp were strong.

Soon, he came upon the outer edges, where sentries sat at the trunks of great beech trees. The blades of their throwing axes glinting in the sunlight that penetrated the canopy. Adolphus was able to skirt around them unseen. The sounds of victorious songs were being sung by the brash warriors who sat around the fire. One such hulking fellow was showing off the heads of three Roman soldiers. He recognised him as the male who coveted his little mate.

Adolphus felt rage building in his heart. He knew the face of one of the heads. It was Claudius - one of his tormentors. Though he was pleased the bastard had gotten what was coming to him, he felt cheated that it had not been him to take the fool's life. Yet the Roman soldier in him knew that vengeance would have been swift. He listened to the boasting of the warrior as the shrubs kept him hidden.

"These Romans! Bah, they're no better than day old pups! We took their scout's camp and burned it to the ground! Their main fortress was a few miles upriver." The warrior took a drink from a skin before clapping a hand on a fellow warrior who sat beside him. "Hallbjörn helped me to push their bodies into the river on a raft, hopefully they'll reach the Roman dog's camp and they'll tuck their tails between their legs and run like bitches back to Rome!" He bellowed with laughter and the other men joined him., Each began to tell a tale of their prowess in battle against the Roman scout's camp. Soon, they finished their tales and began to speak of their plans to join Ariovist's camp

"Ariovist plans for us to cross the river and join his main camp in three days, but if what the Seeresses say is true, we must wait to draw blades against the main army until the new moon." The one who the large warrior had called Hallbjörn spoke as he passed the skin to another warrior.

"Bah, I have never put much faith in the Seeresses," another man lanented. "They said my son would be born healthy and hale, but he was dead from the womb." He spat at the fire. "If it weren't for them, my boy would be beside me right now, boasting about his own battles." The older warrior sighed. "But for those whores." His face was grim as he shook his head and took another draught of mead from the chipped horn.

"My sister has great faith in the Gods, she is even now at Freyja's Tears, preparing for her final trials as a Seeress." The one known as Hallbjörn said.

"Ha! I shall have a great seeress as my wife," the warrior who had slain Claudius boasted.
"I'll be more than happy to have your sister as my bride."

"Be careful she doesn't foresee your prick falling off on your wedding night, Kurst! It may very well come true!" another man teased.

"It won't be falling off, I assure you of that. It will fall inside her and my firstborn son will be conceived that night!" The warrior laughed. "In fact, Halli, your father has promised her to me when we return."

Hallbjörn scowled and muttered under his breath, obviously annoyed by the brash boasting of his friend.

Adolphus felt the hackles on the back of his neck rise and his body tensed as he realised just who the brute, Kurst was speaking of... *his* woman, *his* mate.

He had a duty to Rome. He knew he had to return to his camp and take a report to the hollow tree, but he also wanted to see if his beautiful mate was still safe in the place the warriors called 'Freyja's Tears'

He snuck away from the camp, the fires blazing as the warriors rested for their march to the river, the stench of war behind him as he re-traced his path back to the camp.

She was not there when he returned, but her scent led off in a different direction from where he'd come. He shifted, knowing t her tracks were hours old and led to a bog two miles away where more of their strange totems stood. He moved to the cave and changed into a tunic. The linen felt strange against his skin after walking for so long as a wolf - or naked in the skin of a man, but there was a comfort in them. He could still feel her hands on his body, even if it was a memory in wolf form. There was a connection they both felt and it only strengthened his belief that she was his mate.

Adolphus knew of a few other members of the *Lupus Militari* who were active. Men who he had been raised with, trained to fight beside and served with in Rome's Legions. They were the special units, shunned because of the rumors which insisted they had been touched by the Gods and not in a good way.

Cursed to walk as a man and as a wolf, or so went the versions that travelled around the campfires in the Legion forts where they had been stationed. Over the years, he had lost track of his brothers in wolfskin. He prayed to Mars that they might find their mates as he had found his. Yet, he still didn't have her, he had yet to show her his human form and have her accept him as a man who was also a beast.

Such things played on his mind as he wrote his missive to Legate Valerius. He sealed the parchment, with his detailed report, into the leather tube and then shifted, taking the tube's strap over his head and racing from the cave. His destination - the riverbank where his drop point waited.

Adolphus ran for hours. The stamina of his wolf form was greater than that of his human form which would have collapsed in exhaustion from all his fleet-footed travels over miles of enemy land. One of the advantages of being a wolf under a man's skin.

He placed the leather tube into the hollow tree. The scent of charred and burned leather, wood and dead flesh drifted to him. It was light, distant, but he knew where it was coming from -

upriver! Where the forward scouting camp had been. There was a strong scent of something else, something dead nearby. Adolphus scanned the banks of the river. He shifted back to his human form and approached the steep clay embankment. A headless body, already bloated and grey tinged rested amongst the water reeds.

The remains of a poorly constructed raft lay scattered about the bank. Adolphus slid down the embankment and into the cool waters of the Rhine. He pulled the body to the shore, seeking any marks that might show him who the headless legionary was. The ugly scar on his right shoulder revealed the corpse to be the body of Claudius. Unarmoured, the corpse had bloated and then floated downriver with the remains of the craft that the Suebi, who had slain him, had set him on.

The River was fast flowing in places, but here it slowed. It was a wide place in the river's course and although it took him a while to cross it, he had managed it easily. Adolphus sighed, he was tired of this campaign and wanted nothing more than to settle down on a farm and raise a family. Though he knew his duty was to Rome, he now had something else, something more important to live for. If he could only bring *her* to his side, she would be more important to him than his duty to Rome could ever be. He would be more than happy to leave, to run from Rome's hold on him, so long as she was by his side. Though he was yet to learn her name, he promised himself she would know him soon.

Adolphus sighed as he pushed the body back into the flow of the river. His brother soldiers of Rome would find it when it came upon their fortress by the river's banks a little way downstream. As much as he'd hated the man, Claudius deserved a proper burial, even without his head.

Adolphus' curiosity got the better of him and he headed back upstream in the direction where the scent of smoke and death had drifted from. His wolf senses were strong with his human form, and he was able to follow the littering of bloated bodies and the shattered mockery of funerary rafts that flowed down the river to the site of the burned-out camp.

Adolphus stood on the opposite bank and observed the crows who feasted on the remains of the dead who hadn't floated far from the place of their death. The standards of his Legion were broken, the shafts snapped and the golden standards missing, taken as trophies in the ultimate insult.

He waited and watched a moment longer, before shifting and returning to the forest to head back to his camp and his woman.

Chapter Nine

The scent of mugwort smoke tingled her sense of smell as she sat before the fire. Dusk, had arrived and in the darkening light, Siglind entreated the Gods to grant her a vision, asking for guidance in the final tests for her to enter the next part of her life in the mortal world as a Seeress, like her grandmother.

Siglind had again renewed the protections around her camp, even doubled them with the small bones she'd blessed, left over from the rabbit - the other gift she'd found from the wolf. The meat was drying out over another smaller fire that she'd started with dried peat. The dried meat would add to her dwindling supplies, along with the fish she'd caught in the pool. The fish were drying beside the rabbit and three fresh ones were waiting to be cooked.

Siglind inhaled the smoke, letting it drift over her as she chanted softly, letting herself drift into a meditative state. The veil of the God's sight covered her eyes as she opened herself up to their voices, their visions and their thoughts.

The world was quiet, but for the approach of a warrior. He stood proudly before her, three round and bloodied objects were tied at his belt.

****

"Siglind, I have come to let you know, I intend to claim you as my bride." His voice, strong and safe drifted to her. "I cannot wait any longer, I want you by my side when I return from the war with the Romans. You will be my wife in all ways and give me good, strong boys… our first, we will create tonight."

Her vision blurred between the warrior of her dreams and the man who truly stood before her…

"Kurst…" she whispered as he leaned down, pushing her back until she lay upon the ground. "No!" she cried, struggling as his rough hands gripped her gown and tore at it.

"Yes, Siglind, you tease me to the point of madness with your beauty. Your father has agreed to our marriage."

"But not this way! I refuse you!" She screamed at him as his hands reached down, tearing more of the gown from her body and leaving her naked beneath him. She clawed at him, the last vestiges of the God's veil dissipating with her panic. "Get off me Kurst!" she cried as he lowered himself to her, his lips parted and his rancid breath brushing over her lips as he tried to kiss her. She turned her head away as his lips descended. Kurst gripped her chin in cruel fingers, bruising her skin as he forced his lips to hers. She bit his tongue as it invaded her mouth.

"Bitch!" he cursed as he reared back, his heavy body straddling her. "You'll pay for that, my wife."

"I'm not your wife! I never will be. Gods' curse you, Kurst!" Siglind clawed at his face, her nails connected, digging into his skin and scratching him. He punched her, knocking her near insensate with the blow. Through the fog of pain, disorientation from his strike and the influence of the herbal smoke, she heard him working to remove his clothes, felt the tugging of cloth against skin as he pulled his tunic from his chest. The chill of the early evening breeze caressed her skin.

"Now, lay still, wife, while I fill your belly with my sons." He shifted, undoing his breeches and freeing his cock.

Siglind moaned in pain as her head throbbed from his curt blow. She feebly pushed at him, while the darkness that edged around her vision grew slowly. She could feel herself losing the fight to stay conscious.

In the distance, she heard the growls of an angry animal. A flash of silvery-grey fur flashed past, knocking Kurst to the ground. Siglind fought the darkness and watched as her wolf sunk his sharp fangs into Kurst's arm, savaging the flesh. He screamed, and struck at the wolf, who held on tight, blood dribbling over his grey muzzle. He pushed the wolf off him, the skin and flesh of his arm hung in a bloody mess. Kurst watched the wolf who growled menacingly at the man. Siglind saw Kurst reach for his axe.

She would never allow him to harm her wolf. She drew her small dagger and staggered forward, blade drawn as she pushed herself between the man and the wolf. Kurst was so furious with the beast that he didn't notice her approaching him.

"Hurt him and you'll lose your prick." Siggi's voice wavered with the after effects of the blow to her head and the fear which ran hard and fast through her veins. She pressed the point of her dagger to the base of his now flaccid manhood.

Kurst looked at the near nude woman with surprise, before anger and vengeance blazed in the darkness of his eyes. "Siglind, you'll be mine once the war is over, your father has agreed to it. Then, when I have you in my bed, I'll make you pay. I'll hunt this wolf down and use his head to decorate my shoulders. I'll mount you day and night until my son quickens in your belly, then once he's born, I'll mount you again and again until you bear me another." He yelped when he felt the sharp blade pierce the top of his cock.

"You'll have no cock to give your seed to any woman if you do not leave this place." she glanced down at the three heads attached to his belt. "You have brought three vengeful spirits here to Freyja's sacred place, you are a greater fool than I could have thought! Begone before you befoul the Goddess' sanctuary further!"

Kurst snarled and turned, tucking his now bleeding manhood back into his leather breeches. Siglind kept her blade free and bared at him while beside her, the wolf continued to growl as Kurst retreated back into the forest, mumbling curses at her and the beast beside her.

When Kurst had disappeared from her sight and the wolf stopped growling, she fell to her knees, her head throbbing and her eyesight blurred. Her wolf whined and licked the side of her face, his tail waving miserably at his distress over her state. Siglind put her arms around his soft, warm body and wept. She was so exhausted that she imagined the wolf's fur changing to that of the skin of a strong man. In her distressed haze, she felt herself being lifted and carried over the clearing and into the dark warmth of the cave. Soft shushing noises were made as she was lowered into a bundle of furs. A warm body lay beside her, pulling her into his warmth. Siglind wondered if the Gods had given her an answer, or if she was dreaming again. In truth, she cared not. She felt safe and secure in the arms of her stranger, who had been wolf, but who the Gods had gifted a man's body. A man-beast who cradled her as gently as a babe against his warm, naked body. Within the safety of his arms, she surrendered once more to sleep.

Chapter Ten

Adolphus held his mate in his arms, gazing down at the perfection of her body as she rested. His own warmth radiated against hers as she whimpered in her dreams. He pressed his lips against her temple, the dark bruises on her face blooming in the dim light that suffused the cave. Gently he placed his lips against the blossoming darkness on her skin, trailing kisses down to the softness of her lips. She moaned, wrapped her arms around his body, pressed herself against him. He could scent the sweet tang of her arousal as she gently began to shift her hips against his growing erection. Adolphus looked down at the tiny woman in his arms. Innocent bright blue eyes gazed back at him. Lips, red with the rush of blood were parted as she breathed slowly.

Adolphus watched as his Suebi mate, his beautiful Siglind, pushed him to lie on his back before she shifted between his legs and took his stiffening cock in her soft, gentle hands and began to stroke him. The sensation of her hands against his shaft were pure heaven and the Gods themselves could not have forced him to make her stop. He moaned as he watched her work his sword to hardness in her hands. Her eyes met his briefly, a look of sheer desire burning in them, before her lips parted again and she lowered her head to tentatively touch the crown of his prick in a soft kiss.

Her lips slid over the crown and his head. His body jerked a little as her tongue slid over the underside of his glans, her mouth sucking him as she worshipped his body with her lips and tongue. Adolphus reached down and stroked her head as it bobbed slowly, his body enjoying each wave of pleasure she gifted him with as it washed over him. His groans were filled with passion, but soon, he could bear it no longer.

He pushed her from his crotch, her lips wet and his cock glistened with her saliva. She fell backwards with a gasp and looked at him, a slight trace of fear in her eyes, as she watched him rise over her on his knees. His hand fisted his cock, pumping it a few times, before he placed his large, calloused hands under her bent knees and drew her back towards him as easily as one might draw a blanket over themselves. She gasped as the fingers of one hand made contact with the wetness of her cunny lips. She tried to wriggle away, but he reached around to her backside and pulled her back with a lustful growl. She submitted herself to his fingers, probing and seeking the folds that welcomed his invasion of her sex. She whimpered as he thrust his fingers inside her, his other hand pulling her slightly towards him with each thrust, his digits sinking ever deeper inside her.

She whimpered and writhed under his ministrations, his fingers slick with her arousal and desire. She cried out as her cunny clamped around his fingers, as she gave herself over to her pleasure at his hands. As she caught her breath, he waited, his cock straining forward, desperate to enter her. Her eyes caught his, daring him to take her. He took that dare, positioning himself against her entrance, her hands reaching down to help guide him in. He grunted as he pushed himself inside her slick entrance, his body vibrating with the need to mate with her, to claim her. Her cries, as he began to thrust inside her, were muffled.

Adolphus brought Siglind's body up flush against his chest. She leaned her head against his shoulder as he began to thrust inside her with abandon, their bodies became slick with sweat as they moved against each other, finding pleasure in the body of the other. Their spirits combining, their souls melding together as one.

Siglind cried out her rapture with her head tossed back, as he shuddered beneath her. His lips meeting her collarbone to kiss, nip and lick at the trembling skin. Her body shook with the force of their joining and her breaths panted between her lips with little whimpers. He eased their still-joined bodies back down into the furs that made up his bedding and they lay soaking in the post-climax glow of each other. Siglind's eyes on his. He smiled and brushed an errant strand of her hair from her face. "My mate." he said.

****

"Mate meum." Siglind didn't understand the words he spoke, but she understood the way he held her. Possessive, but loving. Her strange lover's eyes roamed over her body as she lay against him, his member softening within her. She sighed, laying her head against his chest and listened to his heartbeat. If the Gods had sent him to her, then she was a most fortunate woman indeed. His breathing had evened out, his hands stilling in their soft caressing of her naked back. She ever-so-slowly moved out of his embrace, seeking out her discarded clothing. She found it torn and laying in the grass. Her memories flashed back to the evening before.

Kurst had brought harm to her, torn her clothes from her body and attempted to rape her. The wolf... the wolf had come and saved her, then the man had appeared. The man whom she had so willingly given herself to, believing him to be a gift from the Gods. She sighed, there was much for her to work out and interpret from the strange visions.

She looked to the first blushing of dawn as the rising sun lit up the eastern sky with hues of pink, amber, red and finally gold. The orb of fire gave its light to the world and Siglind started to clean up her camp. She needed to find a bone needle and thread to repair the damage Kurst had done to her dress. She found one in her pack and set to stitching back together the rent cloth. She didn't notice the wolf as he left the cave she'd woken in. A short while later, she returned to the cave to find it empty, but for the bundle of furs and a few other supplies her mystery lover had left behind.

She shook out the mended dress and pulled it over her head before she gathered more kindling to restart the campfire. Soon, it would be time for her to join with the war camp.

She gathered herbs and made a tea with their leaves, just as the other wise women of the Suebi entered her camp. Siggi was greeted with sisterly hugs and kisses. Small gifts were given to her to welcome her to the sisterhood of seeresses.ne of the elders sat before her, and gave her blessings.

The women helped her to undress and together they guided Siggi to the waterfall, where, in the crisp, cold waters of Freya's tears, her sisters of the order bathed her, cleansing her as she rose as an inducted Seeress, a wise woman of her tribe. They shared a tea of Mugwort and gave themselves over to their visions.

Siglind saw herself in a strange village, but it was as familiar to her as her grandmother's mud hut. Two children played at her feet - a young boy and a girl with another baby girl perched on her hip and her belly was swollen with yet another babe. She watched as the strange man whom she had shared furs with worked in a field, his hands spreading seeds amongst the hand-tilled earth. He looked up at her and smiled, his ice-blue eyes matched those of the children at her feet.

"Mama! Can I go help Papa?" the eldest boy asked, his eyes pleading with her.

"Very well, Walti, you may, but do as your Papa says." She smiled, reaching down to ruffle the boy's hair before he ran on long, gangly legs to help his father sow the seeds of their winter crops.

She looked down to her middle daughter who smiled up at her before tugging on the skirts of her mother's dress.

"Papa! Wolf!" she cried as she pointed in the direction of her father,.

Siglind looked up to see indeed, where the man had stood, there was now a wolf. Walti ran to the beast and quickly jumped astride the beast's back. With the bag of seeds in hand he began showering the earth, and a little of the wolf's fur, with the seeds.

"Be careful with our son, Adolphus," she called to the wolf.

She received a cheerful-sounding yip in response.

The vision faded and the scent of the smudge stick returned Siggi to her senses. Wendelgard, their elder wise woman nodded at her.

"You are ready, child." She placed a wrinkled hand on Siglind's shoulder squeezing before she rose to her feet, graceful despite her aged bones protesting. "Come, Siglind, Daughter of Adelheid and of Volkmar. We must leave for the war camp. We will be crossing the river within a few days and we must be ready. We will do a final reading of the rods and make sacrifice as needed."

Siggi helped the other women as they broke down her camp. Following them into the forest, she spared a glance back to the cave, where she had laid with the stranger, the man the Gods had sent her. Though she wanted to find him, her duty to her people must come first.

If the Gods willed it, they would meet again.

Chapter Eleven

Adolphus padded through the forest, following Siglind and the other wise women as they made their way to the camp of Ariovist's secondary forces who waited to cross the river. Warriors stood respectfully as the wise women arrived. Adolphus watched as one of the men approached his mate, Hallbjörn, he recalled his name. He watched as he embraced Siglind and walked with her to the hide tents where the wise women had set up.

The scent of many men in a small area assailed his sensitive nose and although he wanted to stay near his mate to ensure her safety, he knew he had his duty to Rome. He slunk away from her, feeling each step grow heavier in his heart.

****

The pounding beat of drums, and the hauntingly beautiful songs of war and glory sounded out around the camp as the gathered warriors made their preparations to go to war against a great enemy. Siglind walked amongst her sisters, all seeresses, her peers. She was one of the youngest women amongst the group, but each greeted her with love and reverence. They spoke of healing techniques and visions late into the evening, when Wendelgard called them all to her tent to share mead and a meal.

"The signs of the willow rods show us the fate of our people if our king does not heed the warnings of the Gods." Wendelgard spoke to the quiet group of women as they huddled beneath fur cloaks for warmth against the cooling evening. "We must keep our faith and sacrifice to the Gods for the King's patience, though I fear he will draw iron and blood before the time the Gods have ordained such things." The older woman, although she was younger than Edda by at least ten summers, cast her wizened gaze over the gathered women.

"Then we must prepare a great sacrifice," one of the other serresses said softly.

"Yes, a great sacrifice. One the Gods demand above all others. One of our brave warriors must give his life in sacrifice to the Gods to temper the King's will.

Siggi held her breath. Human sacrifices were not unheard of within her faith, but she'd seen only two in her life. One no more than a baby, who even Edda knew would not live to see another day, due to a strange shape to his head and a slowness to his movements that no newborn should have. The child's mother had seen the babe was touched by the mad god and had given him over to Edda to return to the Gods.

And now, Siggi would take part in the sacrifice of another life.

"When shall we do this?" the seeress next to her asked softly.

"Once we cross the river and join the King's camp." The elder spoke, her eyes cast over to Siggi. "And our newest acolyte shall conduct the ceremony." Siggi paled. "But the hand of the king shall make the final strike to send the warrior to the gods. As is proper." The wisewoman leaned back against her furs. "Fear not, Siglind, your grandmother will arrive at the King's camp soon after we do. She and I will help prepare you for this honor." She reached out a wrinkled and tattooed hand towards Siggi.

"Thank you, Wise Mother. With the guidance of you and my grandmother, I pray the sacrifice will please the gods and allay the King's eagerness to draw his blade against the Romans." She took the old woman's hand.

"It will be, I have seen it." She released Siggi's hand and turned to the bowl of food which lay at her feet. The women continued to chatter amongst themselves as they ate, although

Siggi's appetite had fled. She excused herself and left the warmth of the elder seer's tent.

The crisp chill of the evening brought a flush to her cheeks as she meandered through the camp. She passed by naked men and women as they writhed together, coupling in the open as the light of the fire bathed their naked bodies in warmth. Musicians played as men danced and sang war songs, others sat and passed the horns of mead around the fires, some chanting or cheering on the couples as they fucked in the firelight.

Siggi moved past the blazing fires and writhing bodies to the edge of the camp. Small totems and trinkets to ward off the evil spirits of their dead enemies hung from poles and posts that had been sharpened and erected into barricades to discourage anyone from forcing their way into the camp.

The mournful call of a wolf echoed through the trees sheltering the camp. Siggi wove her way past the warriors who were on watch.

"Be careful, Seer," one of the men said, his voice gravelly with tiredness. "Wolves are out in the forest this night. The harbingers of the end times sing their own songs of war."

"I will be careful, warrior and I will return if the Gods will it." She pulled the hood of her cloak up over her head, warding against the chill winds that brushed past the branches which lay low on the tree trunks. She walked slowly through the trees until she came to a clearing.

Here, was a small sacred place, set up by the seeresses. Several animal skulls perched on ragged sticks formed a circle, the empty eye sockets glared at her as Siggi lit several torches that were already placed around the clearing. When the circle of skulls was lit with flickering torchlight, she stepped within the circle.

"Wotan, All-Father." s She fell to her knees, arms held wide as she beseeched the God. "Give me the strength to carry out this ceremony which you have demanded. I know I can do this, but I fear it may not be enough. The willow rods have shown me nothing but darkness. What can I do? Please, All-Father, tell me what I can do to return the light to the readings?"

Beyond the circle a twig cracked and broke. Siggi turned, the furs that kept her warm flared out as she spun to face the sound. Her lover stood beyond the circle, light from the torches cast over his naked body. Shadows cast over his face, but the light was reflected in his piercing blue eyes. He raised a hand towards her, stepping into the circle, his lips set into a smile as he approached her.

"Siglind." Hearing her name on his lips shattered her mind. She stepped into his embrace, pulling his body against hers, their lips meeting as she brought his hands to the wooden peg that clasped her fur cloak. His fingers were nimble as he unfastened the peg, letting the furs fall to the earth. She stepped back, her soft leather boots finding the furs at her feet. He watched, mesmerised as she pulled her dress over her head, revealing her nude body in the torchlight. His eyes roamed over her body, devouring her in his sight.

He lowered to his knees before her, hands grasping her hips and pulling her mound to his eager mouth. He gently pushed her thighs apart, opening her for his tongue to explore the place beyond the thatch of curls nestled at the place between her legs. Siglind gasped as his tongue slid between her folds, her soft moans turning to whimpering cries as he found the tiny bud that weakened her knees. With his face still between her legs, tongue sliding over her nub, he helped her to lay down, tugging the furs until they had spread out beneath her back. Siggi's hands found his hair, her fingers ran through the dark curls as he worshipped her with his tongue. She cried out as the pleasure overwhelmed her and her vision blurred from the climax her mystery lover had given her. She lay panting as he rose above her, settling his hips against hers, she could see his erection pressing against her belly.

She looked deep into his eyes - lust, desire, and something else burned in their unfathomable depths. She nodded, breathless at the unasked question. He shifted his hips and with one swift, smooth movement entered her. She whispered a moan, her head tilting back as they joined. His hips moved slowly at first, before he increased the pace, thrusting hard and fast. His grunts, again, were animalistic as he pounded himself against her core. He growled out his climax as his body stiffened above her, her own bliss near-blinding her again as they rode out their pleasure together.

Spent, he leaned down and kissed her, his tongue sliding between her lips to caress her own. He pulled away abruptly, his head turning towards the camp.

"Adprehendet vos ego, mi mate." he whispered, before he pulled himself from her body and left her laying on her cloak, panting, naked and sated. She heard the voices of Hallbjörn and another man in the distance. She dressed quickly and moved to extinguish the torches before her brother came upon her. She gazed around the trees one last time, trying to see if her lover was still nearby.

****

Adolphus turned and watched as Siglind rose to her feet and dressed before she extinguished the torches, casting a last look through the trees. She would not find him, for he lay hidden in a bush, the leaves tickling the fur of his wolf-form.

"I will find you again, my mate." he had said to her before making his escape

He had heard the approach of two soldiers and knew his time with her was short. He had to return to the Legate and made his final report. Time had run out and already some were making preparations for the move across the river. A small group had departed that afternoon, their scents led directly to the river. He'd followed them and found they'd been working on building a small fleet of ferry barges to bring the warriors across the river to join the King's camp. He had made a promise to her and to himself, no matter what happened, he would find her and she would finally be his.

Chapter Twelve.

Siggi moved cautiously through the smoke-haze. The atmosphere around her was thick with anticipation as the camp was broken down and carts were loaded. The snorting of impatient horses and the stamping of their hooves on the soft ground thumped through the pre-dawn grey light that suffused the camp. Fires were extinguished and people rugged themselves up in more furs as the biting cold of the morning buried its way through the layers they already wore.

The older seeresses moved through the groups, offering prayers of safe travels and blessings from the Gods. Word had arrived that King Ariovist had made contact with the Romans and wanted all his people with him, to show the Romans that the answer to their request to leave the lands the Suebi had claimed years ago, was *no*.

The groups moved out one after the other. Word had reached Hallbjörn via their father, who had told Siggi, the rest of their village would be joining them to cross the river. She was eager to see Edda again and tell her of the strange lover who had visited her. She was certain he was a familiar of Wotan, a wanderer, a messenger. But what was the message and why was she so eager to see him again? It felt as though a part of her was missing without him near. She needed to consult with Edda, this felt far too personal to discuss with one of the other seeresses.

She shouldered her pack and walked amongst the people, offering comforting words to the mothers who nursed fretting babes and promises of glory to the warriors who nodded and smiled., She avoided Kurst, whose glare she could feel burning her back. She'd spotted him amongst the warriors of her village, his arm wrapped in bloodied bandages. She had smiled at his misfortune, knowing it was her wolf who had done such damage.

The calls of the ferrymen as they hauled the barges across the river Rhine echoed through the forest as they approached. The smell of campfire smoke and the tang of many sweaty and unwashed bodies permeated the clean scents of the forest as they came to the crossing point.

"Siggi!" a familiar voice called before a small body barrelled into her, his lanky arms wrapping themselves around her legs. "I've missed you!"

Siggi looked down at Ingulf. "Well, hello little warrior!" She smiled, leaning down to embrace him. "I've missed you too."

"Are you a seer now?" he asked.

She nodded. "Yes, I am."

"Can you please tell me my future now?" His eyes pleaded with her.

She glanced around, noticing there was a line for the barges and their turn would come, but not for some time. "All right, let's go find a quiet place and I'll do a reading of the rods."

She took his hand and led him to a small clearing which had yet to be claimed by anyone else who waited to cross the river. She pulled the willow rods from her pouch and took Ingulf's hand as they settled down.

Siggi cleared the leaf litter and sticks from the ground, leaving a bare patch of earth. "Hold these, and think of the question you want to ask the gods." She pulled out some dried sage leaves from another pouch and crumbled them in a circle over the bare earth, hoping to ward off any bad spirits that might cloud the reading.

Ing's little face scrunched up as he thought of the question, his eyes closed tight as if he were wishing really hard. "I'm ready." He placed the willow rods back into her upturned hands.

Siggi clasped her hands together before taking the rods into her right hand and casting them in the air with her eyes closed, they fell to the bare patch of ground with a soft *thunk*. Siggi opened her eyes and her heart sank.

The portent of the willow rods was a bad one, their places spoke of death, darkness and despair. She managed to keep the look of horror from her face. "You will be a great warrior, Ingulf," she said softly, her voice trembling at the last. She had no desire to tell the boy that his first reading might very well be his last. All she could do was lie to save his heart.

"I will?"

"Yes, I have seen it." She spoke with a smile her heart didn't feel.

Ingulf whooped with happiness. He leapt to his feet and hugged her fiercely before running off towards the group where his family waited. Nearby was the litter bearing Edda, she rested on the furs with the other seeresses around her, paying their respects to the wise old woman.

Siglind approached her grandmother's litter and took the old woman's hand. Her skin was cold and weak.

"Edda." She lifted the gnarled hand to her lips and kissed it reverently. "How was your journey?"

"Long and tiring. How much longer till we cross? I need to rest my bones and warm them by a fire," the old woman griped.

Wendelgard approached them. "I have arranged to have us move to the front of the line. We shall board the next barge and cross the river, then continue on to the camp. The Roman army has been sighted by our scouts making their way towards the camp, we must move quickly."

"But the new moon has not risen yet." One of the seeresses spoke from the back of their group.

"I know, but hopefully, Ariovist's seeress can keep his blade from tasting Roman blood. We can only pray to Wotan that he stays the warrior's hand." The women all bowed their heads, each making their own silent pleas to the Gods for temperance as the four warriors who accompanied Edda and carried her litter, hefted her onto their broad shoulders and moved the group to the front of the line.

"When you are rested, Edda, I would speak with you. I have been having strange dreams and there's something else." Siggi spoke softly so only her grandmother could hear.

Edda reached over and placed her hand on Siggi's head. "Of course, child." She shifted slightly on the litter, "When we arrive we shall eat and speak."

The women were loaded on a broad barge with four pole men working to bring their passengers across a section of the Rhine they considered safe to cross. Already groups on the other bank of the river were heading towards Ariovist's camp.

Chapter Thirteen.

"So, tell me, granddaughter, what brings such a sorrowful frown to your face?" Edda asked once they were settled in a hide tent, a brew of warmed mead and herbs and a seed porridge in bowls set before them on the intricately carved small tables they used for meals.

"Many things, Edda. I met a stranger at Freyja's Tears. I don't know, but I think he was a wolf, then he became a man." She held the horn of mead in her hands, letting the liquid warm her as she sipped at it. "We…" she paused, unsure how to continue.

"You made love."

Siggi nodded. "Yes, he saved me from Kurst's unwanted attentions. Kurst brought the heads of three Romans to Freyja's tears. I tried to cleanse the area, but fear the enemy's spirits may have already tainted the sacred place. I willingly gave myself to the stranger, who I believe to be a familiar of Wotan."

Edda was silent a moment as she lay on her furs. "He may be. The Gods have been known to walk amongst men, take brides and lovers and beget children. I pray you are so fortunate." Edda watched Siggi's face carefully.

"There is more?"

"Yes, I saw him again at the last camp only two nights ago. Again, we made love. He spoke to me in a strange tongue I could not understand it."

"The God's words were never meant to be understood fully by mortal men, we can only interpret their will through our divinations."

"That's another thing." Siggi said, her gaze swept over her grandmother's frail body.

"I did a reading of the willow rods for Ingulf. The signs were of death and destruction, but I lied and told him he would be a great warrior."

Edda tutted her daughter's daughter. "Child, I understand your intentions, but to read the willow rods and give a different fate to that which was read is not our place. The fates will be what they will be. It is not up to us to claim any different. The boy may well take what you've said to heart and make a rash choice"

Siggi nodded sorrowfully.

"Well, there is little else you can do, you cannot take back what has been said and now we must speak of other things, of more important things. Wendelgard has told me you will conduct the sacrifice ceremony?"

"Yes, when the moon has been reborn and the time comes for our warriors to draw their swords, I will conduct the ceremony under Wendelgard's guidance."

Edda nodded. "Good, Wendelgard is a powerful seeress, almost as great as I. She will guide you well and teach you many things that I no longer have the time for."

"What do you mean, Edda?" Siggi asked. The old woman was silent. "Edda?"

"Girl, I am tired, leave an old woman to rest." Edda shooed Siggi away.

Reluctantly she cleared the tables, and with the bowls and horns in her hands, she left her grandmother to rest.

Siggi moved amongst her people in the war camp. She walked to the barricades, where from their place atop the hill, she could see the glow of the Roman campfires in the distance. Hallibjörn joined her, a horn of mead in his hand.

"What enemy lies in wait to taste our iron? What glory will be had when we send them to Hell? What treasures will their dead relinquish to our hoard? Come sister, you are a seeress, tell me, what glory have you seen?" He prodded her with a finger.

"Halli," she said, turning to him. "Please, by the Gods, be careful if battle is called. If the war horns sound, you must promise me to take care not to be sent to the otherworld, not just yet." She wrapped her arms around her brother, hugging him tight and resting her head against his chest where she heard the strong beating of his heart. "I fear great darkness will take our people." She felt Halli's hands stroke her hair and shoulders.

"Sister, what do you mean? Great darkness? I don't understand."

"Blades will be drawn, blood will be spilt and only one army will stand…" Siggi gazed out over the grounds that she had seen covered in death. "The blood of the slain shall bring the people to their knees. One man's foolishness will be our undoing." Siggi turned to her brother. She reached up and cupped his cheek with her hand, her thumb sliding over the rough bristles of his beard. "Always heed the wisdom of the Gods, brother." She turned, leaving him to watch the enemy.

When Siggi returned to Edda's tent, the old woman lay still and silent. Her chest did not rise or fall with the rattling breaths which had constantly sounded from her mouth and nostrils. At the touch of her warm hand against Edda's cold skin, Siglind knew her Grandmother had been claimed by Freyja. She reverently folded her grandmother's hands over her chest, one had fallen from the cot she lay upon. Siggi looked down and saw the casting of the rods her Grandmother had done just before her death.

The wolf would save her, but after great cost and misery.

****

The women lamented, wailing to the Gods, asking them to take their sister to her sacred place in the afterlife. Edda lay upon an unlit pyre, her possessions were placed on the woven reed mat beside her. In the house of her afterlife, she would want for nothing. Trinkets, daggers, clothing, all were placed with her on the pyre.

The seeresses chanted softly while behind them, the men stood stoically, their blades wrapped in cloth, their shields on their backs, guarding the earthly body of the old seeress. Siggi accepted a torch from Wendelgard. The wood had been soaked in an oil which would ignite quickly and burn hot, sending Edda's spirit to the afterlife. Siggi chanted, imploring Freyja to take care of her grandmother. Halli stood nearby, watching his sister with pride as she lit the funeral pyre of their grandmother.

The wood caught alight and she stepped back, her brother placed a warm hand on her shoulder and gently squeezed. The crowd dispersed after a short time, some repulsed by the scent of burning flesh, despite the attempts to cover it by burning herbs amongst the pyre. Siggi and Halli stayed, watching as their grandmother's body was given to the flames to turn to ash.

When the ashes had cooled, Siggi took a clay urn from Wendelgard. She carefully and reverently enclosed the skull of her grandmother into the urn and placed all the smaller bones and ashes within the urn. The warped daggers and remains of the trinkets joined the ashes. The remains would be buried after their business with the Romans was done, *if* they survived. The portents were weighing heavily on her mind. She stood and watched the glow in the distance of the enemy fires. The Romans had moved from their fort nearby and now camped in two lines, while one more line of men worked to build another fortified camp.

Siggi moved from the remains of the pyre, the urn with her grandmother's remains cradled against her chest. She prayed their ancestors would watch over them and the Gods would be kind, for she knew their enemy would not be so merciful should they finally attack.

Chapter Fourteen

Kurst smirked at her, his promise to take her as his bride burned strong in his eyes and showed in the arrogant tilt of his head as he joined the raiding party.

The Romans had moved into their new camp and were waiting, for what, was not known, but Ariovist had heeded the warnings of the seeresses and other than small skirmishes which were insignificant and inconsequential, he had not engaged fully with the enemy.

Kurst and Halli were moving out with the rest of the raiding party, their swords had been sharpened and Siggi had helped to conduct a small ceremony, beseeching Wotan for victory. She had re-tied her brother's Suebian knot after the small sacrificial meal they had eaten in dedication to Wotan's good graces. She watched as the men from her village departed.

They returned, hours later, defeated and injured. Hallbjörn was wounded, blood matted his hair from a cut on his scalp and a large gash to his leg. He hobbled, with assistance from another warrior, into the camp. King Ariovist greeted them and demanded a report.

"My Lord, we were defeated, and had no choice but to retreat. We lost many good men in the fighting and some were taken as prisoners."

Ariovist snarled and threw his horn of mead at the fire in anger.

"Will the fools who were captured give our knowledge and the demands of the Gods to our enemies? What do the Gods say now, seers?" he growled, turning his ire onto the wise women. "Do we lay down like tired old sheep to the slaughter? Or shall we roll over, like bitches on our backs, exposing our bellies for the masters of Rome to rub?"

Wendelgard stood, her head bowed respectfully before the King. "My Lord, you must have faith, the Gods will keep their promise of victory, but we must not engage them until the full moon. To go against the wishes of the Gods is pure foolishness."

"Let us see what the next day brings, my Lord," one of his advisors pleaded , trying to bring reason and calm to the angry King's mind.

"Very well, but if Caesar even farts in our direction, I want to be ready to answer with blood and iron, regardless of the Gods' demands!

****

Adolphus had returned to Valerius' camp only to find they had been called to join Caesar's forces at the front against Ariovistus' forces. He arrived at the fort to find a small garrison was holding the place and were interrogating Germanian prisoners. One of them looked familiar. Adolphus stood back and watched as the torture of the prisoners was conducted.

They had been hung, blood trickling from from their wrists, crucified on a frame while the torturer conducted his bloody work.

Their naked bodies had been burned, cut and bruised. All the men were silent in their misery,, although one glared balefully at the Gallic interpreter who was speaking to him.

"What are your King's plans? When will he attack?" the interpreter asked.

The first man spat blood at the man. He received a hard, stunning blow to his ribs for his actions. The torturer moved to the next man - Kurst. The torturer turned to a brazier, wherein iron swords and bars were heating. The ends of the exposed metal glowed red hot as he pulled them from the coals. Kurst whimpered and pissed himself. He screamed before the hot iron even touched him, his words stumbling out as panic set in. The interpreter had asked the same question of him as he had his compatriot. Kurst proved to be both a coward and a traitor.

"The seers! The seers told him the gods won't grant him victory before the full moon!" His scream was piercing as the iron seared his flesh.

This was information Adolphus had in the report strapped to his back. He knew, along with the prisoner's confession and his own scouting reports, Rome had the upper hand and their commanders could make a decision on how to move forward.

"You speak the truth?"

"Yes! Gods yes, I speak the truth. The seers read the signs, the sacred willows blessed by the Oracle. The Gods themselves told them that Ariovist was not to attack until the new moon!" As he cried, blood mixed with his spittle.

The interpreter smirked . "Very good." He clasped his hands together. "Rome is pleased with your words and thanks you for your honesty." He pulled the sleeve of his tunic over his hand and wiped the bloodied spittle that had sprayed on him from the soldier's screaming mouth

"You will die quickly, however, your friends will die slowly, for all your people to witness." He turned to the torturer.

"The Legate will have them hung from the walls." He spun to leave and saw Adolphus standing, watching. "Hail, Soldier."

"Hail. I seek the Legate Valerius."

"He's not here, he has gone to join the rest of the Legion. I'm riding out there shortly to deliver some information. You have a report to deliver?" he asked, eyeing the leather container which held the latest reports.

"I do."

"Excellent, hand it over and I shall deliver them to the Legate myself." The interpreter reached a hand out, fingers wiggling like pudgy worms.

Adolphus knew the type of man who stood before him. The interpreter was the sort who would sell his own mother and sisters to the whorehouse if it meant he would get ahead.

Adolphus had no intention of letting the bastard use him as a stepping stone. Rome was filled with these pompous arses.

"These reports are for the Legate's eyes only. My orders are to deliver them to him myself. I shall ride out with you to the Legion's camp."

"As you wish," the translator sneered.

Adolphus followed him to a group of men who waited to make the mad dash from camp to camp.

Within minutes, they were racing across the field, shouts from the enemy camp sounded and archers stood at the barricades, taking pot shots at them.

They arrived at the wooden palisades surrounding the Legion's camp and were granted entry.

Valerius was in a meeting with Caesar, but excused himself to meet with his scout while the self-important fool hurried to speak with Caesar and deliver the information they'd tortured from the enemy prisoner.

"Sir, I have the final reports. I take it the time to strike is near?" Adolphus handed him the leather package once they'd adjourned to the privacy of the Legate's simple tent. It was far less sumptuous than his pavillion at their old camp.

Valerius nodded. "Yes, we near the final battle with Ariovistus. I'll be glad to see his head fall from his body and be done with this business. I have a wife and mistress waiting for me back in Rome." He sat down heavily. "I hunger for the comforts of home, a nice long soak in the baths or a visit to a *Lupinarium* with good, clean whores wouldn't go astray. I fear the dirt of this accursed land has driven itself in under my skin." He unrolled the parchments and began to skim them with his eyes. Outside, the noise of the Legion mobilising distracted them.

"Hmm, looks like we're preparing for battle." Valerius smiled. "Good." He pulled on his helmet and grabbed his gladius.

"You'll be by my side, Adolphus. I don't trust anyone else in this viper's nest. I swear the battlefield is worse than bloody Rome!"

Adolphus nodded and placed his helmet on his head, tightening the chin-strap so the protective armour was fitting snugly on his head.

The time had come and his thoughts were with his mate. His wolf whined and scratched, wanting to find her and protect her from his fellow soldiers. He knew a woman of such beauty would be highly prized as a slave and many men would relish the chance to break in such a wild spirited woman. He had to find her and take her as his own. It was his only choice.

Chapter Fifteen.

"The Romans are forming ranks!" the scouts shouted from the barricades.

Siglind looked up from her preparations for the sacrifice that was to be held on the eve of the full moon.

"Arm up!" The shout rang through the camp as their warriors rose to the cries to prepare for an attack.

Wendelgard rose to her feet, dusting the earth from her gown. "The King will need to be counselled against attacking the Romans. It is not time and the Gods will not grant us victory if we engage with them." She rushed off to the King's tents, Siglind was but a few steps behind, all her preparations forgotten.

One of his two wives was helping him to dress in his armour as Wendelgard ran up to him. She stood tall and proud as Siglind approached from behind, Wendelgard implored their King to keep his weapons sheathed until the full moon. Siglind watched as the King's face contorted in anger. He grunted in annoyance and left his tent to join the war host, Wendelgard and Siggu were close behind.

"The Gods have abandoned us, the Romans are here, we will destroy them!" He drew his blade and shouted a war cry which was echoed by the rest of the warriors. Wendelgard tried to plead with the king once more, but was forced to step back as Ariovist pushed forward to group up with his men.

Siglind watched as their men moved towards the Roman's ranks. She prayed to Wotan that he would guide Ariovist and their warriors in their battles, if not, then to their places in the afterlife.

"Go, prepare places for the wounded." Wendelgard ordered Siglind, her voice tight with anger. "The king is foolish not to heed the Gods' will, but we must prepare for battle."

Siglind bobbed her head in understanding and ran to the healer's tents where her brother and another man who had been injured in their raid, lay recovering from their wounds.

"Siggi, what is happening?" Halli asked when she entered the tent.

"The Romans are here and they are ready for battle. King Ariovist has ordered the warriors into formation and is going to meet them. The Romans are so close you could spit on them."

"Give me my sword." Halli sat up, pushing the furs and blankets from his body. The wounds on his scalp had scabbed over and were healing, but his leg was still far from being healed.

"No, brother, you are still wounded." She looked over the bloodied bandages which were wrapped around his thigh.

"I won't lie here like an old man waiting for death, Siggi."
Halli snapped, the bloodlust burning in his eyes. "I'll die with a
sword in my hand and the enemy's blood painting my skin."

The war horns sounded, then another horn, unfamiliar in
its tone and from beyond their tent, they heard the sounds of a
battle joined.

"Halli, please." Siggi begged her brother. . Hallbjörn
grunted as he pushed himself to his feet.

"Siglind, I am a warrior. If today will be my death, I'll
greet it on my feet and defending my people. Now, give me my
sword, Sister."

Siggi pushed to her feet and gathered his sword and
armour. She helped him to dress and handed him his sword.
Before she let go of the hilt, he gripped her wrist with a strength
that spoke of a powerful warrior, though the beading of sweat
already on his forehead spoke of how much pain he was truly in.

"Promise me, if they break through our lines, you will take as many women and children as you can and escape to the river. Get across it and return to our ancestral lands in the north." He gripped her hand harder. "Promise me."

Siglind nodded. "I promise."

Halli pulled her in for a close embrace, kissing her hair before he pushed her gently away. "I love you, Sister. If the Gods will it, I will return."

"Be careful brother." Siggi watched as her brother moved to leave the tent. "And, may the Gods be with you on this day of battle."

In her heart, Siglind knew she would never see her brother alive again.

****

The men had been fighting for hours. The stench of blood and death permeated the air as blades flashed and the blood of warriors, both Roman and Germanic, splattered the ground.

They'd broken the Germannian's right flank and had managed to surround their main forces. Some enemy warriors began to flee back towards the enemy camp.

"I can tell that you want to join the fight, Adolphus." Valerius smirked from beneath his helmet. "Take a group of men and find us some slaves. I think women and children would be a good start."

"Yes, Legate." Adolphus gathered together a group of reserves and they ran around the main force of the now dying battle, the cries and groans of men as they lay wounded and dying gave the battlefield a more horrific ambience. As they neared the side of the enemy encampment, they could see chaos was reigning as the non-combatants of the camp rushed to gather belongings and make their escape.

There was a group of women and children rushing to the back of the camp and leading them was the familiar face of his mate. His wolf scratched at the cage of man. He soothed it with the promise that he would have her and soon. What they would do after, he didn't know, but something told him his time in the Legion was almost up. He knew he would never be released from his service, being a member of the *Lupus Militium*. He and Siglind would have to run, but until that time came, he still had his duty.

"Let's head them off before the river," he ordered the men. They ran through the nearby forest, branches and scrubby bushes scratching at their legs as they moved swiftly to get ahead of the fleeing group. They watched and waited until they heard the sobs and cries of a distressed group of women and children. They entered a clearing near Adolphus' position and the children, exhausted from their long run flopped down to rest.

"Spread out and surround them, but wait for my signal to close the trap." he whispered to the group of men.

They moved quietly, the cries of despair covering much of the movement of heavily armoured men as they shifted into positions through the forest surrounding their little clearing. His eyes stayed on Siglind as she wandered through the forlorn group and checked on everyone, including a pregnant woman. His heart beat faster as she spoke with a small child, the child took her hand and rose to his feet. They moved towards his position.

Chapter Sixteen.

Siglind looked over the bedraggled group of women and children. Back in the camp, Wendelgard approached her, fear in her eyes.

"We have lost, the Gods wrath has come down upon us. Run, take as many women and children as you can. Get back across the river and rest at Freyja's Tears then, move on to the northlands where our people are. You will find sanctuary there." Wendelgard handed her a bundle of healing herbs, wrapped in goatskin. "Take these, you will need them. Use the wisdom of the Gods to guide you, Siglind." Siglind had nodded and thanked the elder wisewoman before she'd gathered a group of frightened women and children and made their escape.

Now they rested in a clearing, the children were crying, some of the mothers were as distraught as their children. One woman, who waa heavily pregnant, was struggling to keep up. Siglind's hands and arms were bloody from helping with the wounded as they'd poured back to camp during the battle. In the healer's tents she'd received word of her father and brother's deaths.

One of the children needed to relieve himself, so she took him to some of the trees surrounding their clearing. Once he was done, she took him back to the group and checked over her charges. While she soothed the crying children, she felt as though she was being watched.

Her dress bore the marks of battle and her spirit was waning. She left the group, heading into the forest and took a moment to do a quick casting of the willow rods. What she saw was very troubling.

There was the sound of a stick breaking underfoot and she looked up, expecting it to be one of the children, perhaps come to relieve themselves amongst the trees. She was met with the piercing eyes of the man whom she'd given her body to, her wolf-man wore the armour of a Roman Legionary.

"No…" she cried, her heart breaking as she stumbled backwards, falling to the forest floor when a fallen branch caught her legs.

He reached out for her, his voice soft as he spoke to her in her language. "Be calm, beautiful Siggi. I must take you and the others captive and return with you to my camp. I'm sorry."

"I trusted you. I thought you were…" she stopped. In truth she didn't know who he was, or what he really was. She tried to scramble backwards, his hand grabbed her leather-booted foot and held her, his eyes catching hers as she glared at him.

"I am a scout for the Roman Legion, Siggi. I was sent to scout out your camps and report back to my people… but, I am also-"

"You are a liar and a traitor to my heart," she screamed out, cutting his words off. Kicking at his face with her free foot, he easily caught it. Leaning forward, he placed a knee over her legs, keeping her pinned. She grabbed a handful of leaf matter and threw it in his face, her fingers curled and nails scraping across his cheek. He spat the dirt that entered his mouth and grabbed her hands, pinning them together above her head. Adolphus reached into a small pack on his belt and withdrew some leather strips, binding her hands with them.

Through the forest, where the others rested, their cries and screams of fear echoed. Siggi turned towards the sound, but in her bound state she could do nothing. "No! They are innocents, women and children who are no threat to Rome, Let them go, please…" she begged, turning to face her lover, her captor.

"They won't be hurt." Adolphus said. "So long as they cooperate." He hauled her to her feet.

She felt hot tears of betrayal burning her eyes, to escape and trickle down her cheeks.

"Shh, sweet one. I'm going to claim you as my own and then, we'll return to Rome." He reached up and stroked her cheek gently. "You will be safe under my protection."

"I would rather die than go to your Rome. I am not a Roman and never will be!" she spat, defiantly.

"I know, but the fates have given us to each other, surely you feel it too? His hands caressed her body as she fought him.

She slowly began to relax as he stroked her into submission. Her hot, angry tears still trickled down her cheeks and he carefully wiped them away.

"Siggi, I cannot live without you. You are my mate. There is so much I have to tell you, so much for us both to learn, but I need you to trust me, please?"

"I can't, you betrayed me. You never told me your name."
She turned her head away from him, unable to look at him.

"It's Adolphus." He turned her face back to his, his eyes
searching hers for a speck of forgiveness and finding none.

He reached up to brush some errant strands of hair from
her face when a woman's scream from the clearing broke their
gazes. "Come, something's amiss." He pulled her along, her feet
stumbling a little on the uneven ground as they reached the
clearing. A Roman soldier stood above the body of a young child,
his sword dripping with crimson blood.

"Ingulf!" Siggi cried out in despair, broke free of
Adolphus' grip and ran to the boy.

His eyes were glassy and his face so innocent in its youth.
Clutched in his still hand was a small bronze dagger, used by the
seeresses in the ceremonial sacrifices of small animals. He must
have taken it from her pack. Her predictions had come to pass.
Ingulf had died far too young.

She felt her anger rising. "Is this what Rome does to its captives? Slaughtering young children who seek only to defend their people?" She rose to her feet, her bound hands curling into fists. "Rome will be sent to Hel for what they have done to our people. This is not your land!" She screamed at the Romans, but only Adolphus understood her words. He placed a hand on her shoulder as she broke down, weeping over the boy's body. Between sobs, she sent a prayer to Freyja to take the boy into her care, beseeching her beloved Goddess to protect them from the wrath of the Romans.

She felt Adolphus' hands pull her gently from Ingulf's still-warm body, blood from his wound joining that of the other warriors on her gown, staining it.

As Adolphus led her and the others away from Ingulf's body, she felt the despair that the Gods had truly abandoned the Suebi this day.

****

They walked for hours, stopping to rest every so often, until they arrived at the closest camp - Valerius' camp. Cohorts began to return, battered, bruised and bloodied. Adolphus set Siglind in with the other Slaves, registering her with the scribes as a captured slave. Rome's bureaucracy still held firm, especially in wartime. He would place a request with the Legate to take her as a war prize for his services as soon as the Legate returned. Until then, he bathed and made sure that Siggi and the other captives had eaten. He lay down on his pallet and closed his eyes, he had much to plan and do, yet sleep captured him and pulled him deeply down in its embrace.

When he awoke, he went to check on Siggi. The slaves huddled away from him like frightened animals in their pen, but Siggi was nowhere to be seen. He asked the slavemaster where the golden haired woman had gone.

"Oh, her? There was quite a lot of interest in that one, but you're too late, soldier. The Legate has claimed her." He spoke with a smirk on his face.

Adolphus turned and strode quickly to Valerius' pavillion, he hoped he was not too late to try to convince his Legate to give him back his mate.

Chapter Seventeen.

The man who stood before her in simple linen robes was disgusting. Heavyset, with muscle running to fat, he had a putrid odour that spoke of rotting teeth and a man who barely bathed.

She was bound to the central post holding his pavillion up. His rough hands had explored her curves as she struggled against her bonds. A shining dagger had cut through the bloodied dress she'd worn and now she stood naked, bound and at his mercy. She spat at him when he cupped one of her breasts, the resulting strike to her face had left her stunned and another bruise was most certainly forming on her cheek. She bore his rough hands, all the while praying to Freyja for death

Adolphus' promises of protection had been nothing but dust on the wind. She knew she should never have trusted him. She hissed with disgust as the man, Valerius, shoved his filthy hands between her legs. If she ever got free, she'd happily sacrifice him to the Gods and shove his headless corpse into the bogs for good measure.

She looked up as the light in the tent turned from dim to blinding as someone entered.

"Ah! Adolphus!" the foul man said.

Then she struggled to understand what he said to the man she despised most at that moment. Their tongue was strange, lilting, unlike the rough and gutterral words of her own people. Adolphus muttered something back to him. She flinched when Valerius reached out and pinched a nipple. Adolphus' face contorted in anger and he drew his sword as the Legate kept his eyes and groping hands on her breasts.

The Legate's head was cut cleanly from his shoulders and his blood spurted from his severed neck, coating her face, naked chest and belly before Adolphus gripped the foul and now very dead Roman under the armpits and lowered him to the ground quietly so as not to alert the guards who stood just outside the man's tent. Adolphus looked up at her with regret in his eyes as he stood and moved behind her. "I am so sorry, my mate, for what has happened today."

He worked the knots free of the leather ties binding her hands and feet. She ran to a bowl of water and quickly washed the blood from her face and chest, turning to see Adolphus approaching her with a cape to cover her nakedness.

"We will have to leave, I will be killed for murdering my Legate if I am caught and they may kill you too." He wrapped her in the linen cape and held her close against his body, his voice was low and whispered.

"I won't leave without my people," she whispered back, defiant in her decision.

"What can we do? Short of killing or getting the entire camp to sleep…"

"I can help. There are plants and mushrooms in the nearby forest that will make them sleep, if we can get them into their food or water…"

"We can escape." He nodded. "You'll need to trust me."

"No, it is you who will need to trust me, Adolphus. Once we cross that river, you are in my lands. Gods know I am in your debt for what you have done, though I believe we are close to even." She reached up and caressed his face. "I thought you had abandoned me." She glanced at the headless body, before her eyes swept back to his, the light of love shone brightly within their depth, despite all that had happened between them.

"I was late because I fell asleep and for that I am sorry." He pressed a kiss to her soft lips, pulling her close against his body. The scent of her almost drove his wolf crazy, but they both knew their time was limited. "I wish I could show you how much I love you and need you right here, right now, but we are running out of time." He pulled away from her, the heat of his body already missed. "Can you help me to get his body onto the bed? We need to make it look like he is resting."

"Would it help if I cried and screamed as well, make it sound as though you are both taking me?" she asked, grabbing the dead man's feet.

"Maybe." Adolphus said with a grunt. "Then perhaps the guards will know not to disturb us…"

Siggi mock-cried and whimpered while Adolphus grunted as if he and the Legate were both raping her. They managed to get the body onto the bed and covered with woven blankets and furs, before Adolphus found his severed head under a table and placed it on the pillows. He then led Siggi out of the tent, grunting to the two soldiers in their language. She kept her head bowed and hobbled along as though she'd been roughly taken by two men.

Adolphus led her to the edge of the camp and beyond, into the forest where a small stream ran. He helped her to gather the fungi and plants that would bring the camp to its knees.

They returned with a bundle of the potent fungi. Siggi returned to the Legate's pavillion where she grabbed what food she could and prepared to travel, while Adolphus dropped a few of the fungi into each cooking pot. The warriors soon began dozing off after eating.he entire camp, with the exception of Siggi and the other captives had eaten the poisoned meals. Once they were all down, Adolphus collected Siggi. The two guards had been fed the same meal as the warriors and were asleep by the time he arrived. The camp was eerily quiet, but for the snores of the men. The captured women and children still huddled in their pen. Siggi ran to them, having donned one of the Legate's simple tunics which hung very loose on her.

"Come, while they sleep, we must run."

The others eyed Adolphus warily. He wore the red tunics of a Roman soldier.

"Can we trust him?" one of the women asked as she held a small child close.

"Yes." Siggi smiled at Adolphus. "We can, he is chosen by the Gods. When the time is right and we are safe at home, I will take him as my husband."

"Come, we must go." Adolphus opened the pen.

The others ran out, eager for freedom. "Gather what you can, but do not eat the stew, it will make you sleep," Siggi warned.

Adolphus looked at Siggi, her eyes shone with unshed tears.

"We will be alright, my love." He spoke the words as his hands reached to caress her face, being mindful of the blossoming bruise Valerius had gifted her with.

"I know, Adolphus. The Gods told me so."

Chapter Eighteen.

Five years later.

Siglind watched as Adolphus worked the plow. His bare back glistened with sweat. The children at her skirts watched their father as he cleared the ground for a new planting season. One at hip, two at feet and yet another in her belly.

Their small village had been blessed by the Gods. They had run for weeks until they found the site where Siggi had done a casting of the willows and had gained the Gods favour. The soil was rich and black, the small river that ran nearby graced them with clean, clear water from the not-too-distant mountains. Here they thrived, Adolphus had helped them to set up farms and a small road system that ran between their homes.

At her feet, their eldest tugged at her skirts.

"Mama, may I go help Papa?" he asked.

"Of course, Walti, just be careful." she smiled, ruffling the boy's hair. On her hip, their youngest shoved a fist into her mouth, letting the dribble run down her chin until Siggi noticed and wiped it away with the sleeve of her dress.

"Your teeth are coming in, I think, little Edda." she cooed to the little girl. She kissed her precious daughter on the cheek. "Come, Halli, let's go start dinner."

"Papa, Wolf!" little Halli cried out, pointing to the field. Siggi turned and watched as Walti climbed on the back of the grey wolf's back.

"Adolphus!" she called. "Take care of our son!"

She heard him chuff in understanding.

Though her vision was slightly different from the reality, Siggi knew her vision had now come to pass.

The Gods had blessed her, though it was not without great sacrifice.

Her family and most of her people were now dust and bones, memories in her heart.

Word had reached them from travelling merchants that the Romans were moving through the Germanic lands.

Her last casting had shown her that one day, the Romans would be here too.

One day.

But not today.

www.ingramcontent.com/pod-product-compliance
Lightning Source LLC
Chambersburg PA
CBHW070014140726
47908CB00020B/1365